Sage Carrington

Math Mystery in Mexico City

Justin Scott Parr

D1165956

GumshoePress

Text copyright © 2014 Justin Scott Parr
Illustrations and artwork copyright © 2014 GumshoePress

Editor: Carrie White
Cover Art by: Igor Adasikov, Afreena Rahman
Cover Design by: Svetlana Uscumlic, Kath Grimshaw
Interior Design by: Susan Veach

ISBN: 978-1-939001-59-7 (Paperback)
ISBN: 978-1-939001-22-1 (Electronic)

Books may be purchased in bulk at special discounts for promotional or educational purposes. Inquiries for sales, distribution, and permissions should be addressed to:

GumshoePress
P.O. Box 458
New York, NY 10027
support@gumshoepress.com
www.gumshoepress.com

For all the "Sages" in the world.

Chapters

1   Ready for Departure   1

2   Sunrise at 40,000 Feet   15

3   The Miracle Hotel   21

4   Beatriz the Angel   29

5   The Blue House   35

6   Frida's Secret   49

7   Bedtime Decryption   53

8   Morning in Mexico   68

9   A Tour of El Zócalo   77

10   Pyramids at Teotihuacan   88

11   Lessons from the Olmecs   96

12   Izzy's Party   110

13   Midnight Development   122

14   Cracking the Cipher   128

15 In the Castle's Shadows 137

16 Constant Change 144

17 Abril and Fernando 154

18 Journey to the Aquarium 157

19 10,000 Millimeters Under the Sea 161

20 A Breath of Fresh Air 171

21 Wisdom, Love, and Illumination 175

22 Beyond the Surface 186

23 Return to Casa Azul 192

24 Message on a Flagpole 199

25 Frida's Final Words 203

26 Airport Dash 209

27 Race to the Gate 212

28 Ready for Arrival 216

1

Ready for Departure

Countless stars peppered a moonless sky, and the flashing transponders of distant airplanes seemed to bounce around the constellations like a galactic game of pinball. A jumbo jet roared overhead and descended onto the runway. Its tires squealed and released a puff of smoke upon touching the pavement.

Sage mashed her face against the terminal's window. *I can't wait to fly,* she thought. *I wonder where all those planes are coming from? Probably Paris, Tokyo, Los Angeles, Cairo ...*

Another jet rumbled overhead, its landing gear reaching for the earth. "Boy, that one sounded close!" she said. "Hey, Izzy, did you see the smoke when it landed!?"

Click. Click.

Isabel lowered her camera, then gave it a few

loving taps. "Yep, captured it all right here." She looked toward the sky. "Although it's pretty dark out there. No moonlight or anything. Hope I got the shot."

Sage pointed to the back of Isabel's camera. "How do you ever know if you got the shots, Izzy-dactyl?" *It's a film camera,* she thought. "There's no screen on the back."

"I just know, Sage-asaurus. But now that you mention it … in this low light, I probably need a faster lens." Isabel reached into a red backpack with thick black letters stamped on its front: *End of World Kit.* She placed several items on the floor: candles, first-aid kit, bottled water, can opener, magnifying glass, scissors, tape, and a sewing kit.

Always be prepared, Sage imagined Isabel saying. Ever since they had met six years ago, in the second grade, Isabel had been obsessed with planning for earthquakes, alien invasions, and nuclear fallout. Sage found her best friend's preoccupation with natural disasters endearing and always felt safe with Izzy nearby.

She also knew that Isabel's emergency kit could come in handy for their upcoming journey. After all, the best friends were moments away from departing for Mexico City. Isabel had already traveled there a few times; her family was originally from Veracruz, a town on Mexico's gulf coast. However, this would be Sage's first time outside of the United States, and she was thrilled to explore a new place.

The girls had only found out last week that they were even going to Mexico. That was when their parents—all researchers with the Smithsonian Institution—discovered that their support was needed at several archeological sites around that country. Sage's parents were physical scientists, and Isabel's parents specialized in natural and social sciences. As members of the Smithsonian's newly-created International Consortium of Scientific Research, they were responsible for collecting and analyzing field data at historic sites around the world. Fortunately for Sage and Isabel, the institute's funding came through just as the school year ended, so they would be able to travel with their parents during summer break.

Sage returned Isabel's emergency items to the backpack. "You have everything you need?"

"Always be prepared," Isabel said while switching lenses on her camera. "It's hurricane season, you know. But don't worry; we're ready for the big one."

"Don't jinx me!" Sage said, thinking about the SCUBA dive she had planned for their third day in Mexico. She'd been working toward her Open Water Diver certification in Washington, DC and had already planned to complete her final dive in the Chesapeake Bay. But after her parents learned about the trip to Mexico, they agreed it would be exciting for her to take her fifth dive at one of the top sites in the world. "We're supposed to have perfect weather in Cozumel on Friday. Sunny, warm, and clear skies. I've already checked the forecast ... five times!"

"Well, it's only Tuesday, so a lot could change, you know?" Isabel tinkered with her camera's dials. "This is all just in case, Sage-asaurus."

"Yeah, I guess." She grabbed a seat next to Isabel and fanned through several pages of a yellow paperback book. "Hey Izzy, did I tell you I decrypted another one?" She chuckled to herself. "This one's a joke. Want to hear it?"

Isabel started giggling as if she'd already heard the setup and the punch line. "Tell me!"

"Okay, hold on a sec. I wrote the plaintext inside the *Book of Love*." Sage retrieved a decorated journal from Isabel's backpack. The book's cover displayed a collection of stickers scattered around a hand-drawn title: *Sage & Isabel's Book of Love*. The girls shared the journal and filled its pages with personal notes, archived photos, science experiments and, most recently, secret codes.

Sage flipped through several pages. "Here it is!" She cleared her throat. "Okay ... if you're American in the kitchen ... and you're Australian in the living room ... then what are you in the bathroom?"

Isabel thought for a moment while mumbling the question to herself. "I don't know. I give up."

"European!" Sage noticed Izzy didn't catch the joke. "Get it? *Eur-a-pean.*"

"Oh wait!" Isabel fell against Sage as the two girls melted into a ball of laughter. "You're a peein'!"

"Nefertari Sage Carrington!" her mom said. The girls spun around and saw Mrs. Carrington with one hand on her waist and the other holding a small camera. "Careful, young lady."

"What?" Sage said, as innocently as the guilty can be. "I only said 'European.'"

Mrs. Carrington smirked and shook her head. "Where do you girls even get this stuff?"

Sage walked over to her mom and extended another book. "From here." A collection of question marks and strange letters filled the cover, along with the title *101 Codes, Cryptograms, Ciphers, and Other Mysterious Messages.*

"Don't think I've seen this one before," Mrs. Carrington said. "Cryptograms?"

"Yes, Mommy, they're secret messages based on different combinations of letters, numbers, shapes—"

"Or symbols," Isabel added. "And they can be arranged in different patterns. Some are simple like rail-fence, twisted path, and date shift—"

"Yeah, those are all basic substitution ... super easy. But other patterns take more time to crack, like Playfair and digraphic. Those are polyalphabetic—"

"That means each letter in the code can be represented by multiple symbols."

"Those ciphers are way harder!"

"Ciphers?" Mrs. Carrington asked.

"That's just another word for cryptogram, Mommy. That's the secret message. Look." Sage turned the book's pages; nearly all were dog-eared and scribbled on. "Then after we *decipher* the message, we write down the decoded *plaintext*."

"Yeah, Mrs. C, plaintext is the *answer* to the cipher."

Mrs. Carrington seemed amazed at the girls' interest. "And you solved all these?"

"Yep," Sage said. "We're real code breakers!"

"That means we'll definitely get the cryptography questions correct on the astronaut's exam," Isabel said. "Well, if there *are* any."

For as long as Sage could remember, she and Isabel had shared the same dream—to blast into space and explore the planets and the solar system. They aspired to become real live astronauts. "For sure, Izzy. We'll ace those."

"Have you girls ever seen a puzzle you couldn't decipher?" Mrs. Carrington fanned through the book's pages. "Looks like it's time to find a harder cryptogram to solve."

"Bring it on!" Izzy said.

Mrs. Carrington returned the book to Sage. "I want a picture of you two. Here." She handed each girl a small blue booklet. "Hold up your passports."

Sage examined the document's cover; its coarse texture felt like a combination of plastic and sandpaper. The words *United States of America* were printed across the bottom with *PASSPORT* at the top. She flipped through the booklet and arrived at a page with her name—Nefertari Sage Carrington—along with a photo. "Cool! Izzy, do you see the picture?"

Isabel was staring at the same page of her passport. "We look so ..."

"Official!" Sage added.

"Super official!"

"Like we're with some agency." Sage held up her passport. "My name is Sage Carrington, and—" She flipped the passport open as if it were an FBI badge. "I'll need you to step away from the Space Shuttle."

"Yeah," Isabel said, playing along. "There are only two more seats on this lunar mission, buster... and guess who's gonna get 'em."

The girls burst into laughter as Mrs. Carrington raised her camera. "Okay, let me see your passports. Hold them up." She lowered the camera. "Give me a *real* smile, Sage, not that fake one."

At five o'clock in the morning, Sage thought, *this is as real as it gets.*

Mrs. Carrington returned the camera to her eye. "That's better."

Click. Flash.

Mrs. Carrington glanced at the back of the camera and nodded. "That'll be a good one for the *Book of Love*." She looked at Sage and Isabel. "You want to see?"

"Yes!"

"Of course!"

Mrs. Carrington extended the camera, and both girls huddled around the digital image. In the picture, Sage and Isabel stood inside the bustling airport terminal, toothy smiles on their faces. Sage's braces sparkled in the light, and they both clutched a passport in one hand. Isabel's other arm was wrapped around Sage's waist, and Sage clenched *101 Codes, Cryptograms, Ciphers, and Other Mysterious Messages*. Their mismatched sandals showed colorfully painted toenails—also mismatched. Above the girls' heads, a large sign hung from the rafters: *International Departures*.

"And I see you're taking the shoe-swap on the road," Mrs. Carrington said, referring to the girls' mismatched footwear.

Whenever they were shopping for Sage and Isabel, their moms coordinated to purchase the same shoe style—but in different colors. Before leaving the store, Sage's mom swapped one shoe with Isabel's mom. This routine ensured that both Sage and Isabel would have a mismatched pair of shoes.

"Of course, Mommy," Sage said. "It's our bestie style."

"Yeah," Izzy added. "Well, as long as our feet stay the same size!"

"Enjoy it while you can." Mrs. Carrington glanced at her watch. "We should be boarding the plane shortly, kiddos. Make sure you have everything ready to go."

"We're ready, Mommy."

"Yeah, Mrs. C, *estamos listas.*"

Mrs. Carrington winked, hugged the girls, then strolled across the waiting area to join Isabel's mom. They stood in front of a wall-sized window overlooking the runway, while chatting, joking, and carrying on. For a moment, Sage imagined that one day, many years from now, that's exactly how she and Isabel would act. A couple of grown women, still best friends after all the years.

She scanned the waiting area. A collection of luggage, sleeping kids, and adults surrounded her. Sage's friend, Benjamin Woodson, stretched out across a sleeping bag on the floor; the eleven-year-old was out like a light. Nearby, Aunt Drusilla was reading a small phrasebook while practicing several Spanish expressions out loud.

Mr. Flores paced the floor while talking on the phone. Sage understood a few of the Spanish words in the conversation. "*Sí, Mama,*" he said. "*Vamos a salir en unos minutos. Vamos a verte pronto. Isabel? Sí, claro. Ella ésta crescendo muy rapido. Con certeza. Te amo.*"

Not far from Mr. Flores, Sage's dad was engaged in the morning newspaper. It was a familiar sight. Mr. Carrington's arms were extended, holding the paper open like a wall poster. Sage was always amazed at how her dad seemed to know so much about so much. *Read the newspaper every day*, she heard his voice say. *Even if it's just one section. Read every single day.*

As she walked toward him, she smiled while thinking of the conversation they'd had regarding *Binary and Little Bits*, Sage's favorite musical group. Her dad had shared details about the group's small-town roots, favorite cities to play in, and even the musical artists who inspired them. Many of these details Sage didn't even know. For a man with taste in classical and jazz, she wondered how her dad could have possibly known about an indie rock band comprised of high schoolers.

"Read every single day," she whispered to her dad before inching closer and kissing him on the cheek.

"Hey, princess," he said. "I thought you'd be

resting." He lowered the paper, then scanned the area. "And Isabel, too. You girls didn't sleep all night."

"Too anxious." She looked at an electronic sign behind her dad: *MEXICO CITY—ON TIME.* "I just want to get there already!"

"I know what you mean," he chuckled. "Exciting, isn't it?"

"Super exciting."

Isabel walked over, plopped down beside Sage, and leaned in.

"But, honey," Mr. Carrington said, "you should rest. And you too, Isabel. We have a full itinerary today."

"What's an *itinerary*?" Sage asked.

"That's our schedule," Mr. Carrington said.

Isabel wrapped an arm around Sage's shoulders. "What's on our ... *itinerary*, Mr. C?"

Mr. Carrington folded the newspaper. "Let's see. We have a four-hour flight from Dulles to Mexico City, so we'll arrive later this morning. The Smithsonian has arranged our accommodations. The hotel's in the middle of the city. Lots nearby for you to see and do—museums, statues, monuments." He touched Sage on the nose as he added, "And the Blue House."

"*¡Casa Azul!*"

"Frida Kahlo!"

11

Sage and Isabel were enamored with the strength, courage, and individuality of Mexico's famous female painter. They had researched Frida's difficult life— the bus accident that nearly killed her at eighteen, and the decades of sickness and pain that came after. They knew of her tumultuous marriage to Diego Rivera, and had also studied her amazing paintings that depict a raw perspective on humanity. And, on top of all that, the girls absolutely adored Frida's style. They were captivated by her hair, dresses, blouses, and jewelry. The unibrow across her fore-head. Even the hint of a mustache above her lip. Frida was unique, just like Sage and Isabel. In fact, and they would *never* share this secret with anyone, the girls' mismatched shoe-swap was a tribute to the spirit of Frida Kahlo.

"She's our hero." Isabel motioned to her parents. "And you guys wondered why we couldn't sleep last night."

"Yeah, Daddy, Frida's all we can think about."

"She passed away many decades ago," Mr. Carrington said, shaking his head in wonder. "Nonetheless, it appears that Frida Kahlo still holds the hearts and minds of at least two twelve year olds from Washington, DC."

"We won't be twelve much longer. Izzy's on her final day."

"Yeah, Mr. C, and Sage is in her last week!"

"What else is on our itinerary, Daddy?"

"Well ... tomorrow is a big day." He placed a hand on Isabel's shoulder. "We're celebrating the birth of a Gemini—"

"Izzy!"

Isabel smiled. "The party's in Veracruz, Sage. You'll meet my aunt and uncle ... oh, and my cousins Escarlet and Victor!"

"Can't wait!"

"We're all excited about your party, Isabel," Mr. Carrington said. "But before Veracruz, we're traveling north of Mexico City, about thirty minutes, to Teotihuacan."

"The pyramids!" Sage said.

Her dad nodded. "And then southeast to San Lorenzo for the Olmec site."

"The Olmecs ... those are the giant stone heads, right?"

"Yes, princess. We'll be there tomorrow afternoon."

A speaker hissed above their heads, and a voice filled the terminal. "Flight 1216 to Mexico City will begin boarding shortly. Again, 5:30 a.m. flight 1216 to Mexico City will board shortly. Please have your boarding passes out and ready for the gate agent."

"Get your things together, kids," Mrs. Carrington said as the group scrambled to gather their belongings.

13

"I have all the boarding passes," Drusilla said.

Sage's stomach tightened as she imagined her first international flight. *In a few minutes,* she thought, *we'll be in the air. And in a few hours ... Mexico City.* She tapped Isabel on the shoulder. "This afternoon, Izzy, we'll be face to face with Frida!"

The girls extended their pinkies, locked them together, and shook. A surge of fatigue suddenly struck Sage, and she yawned loud enough for the whole line to hear. Isabel mimicked her best friend, as their mothers spun around.

"Isabel!"

"Sage," Mrs. Carrington added, "was that you?"

The girls looked at each other and smiled. Sage shrugged. "Maybe we should have slept a little last night."

"Well, you girls can snooze for a few hours on the plane," Mrs. Flores said.

Sage smiled at the gate agent as the group strolled past an electronic sign: *MEXICO CITY— ON TIME. Well*, she thought, *here we go.* "*Vamos*, Izzy-dactyl."

"*Claro*, Sage-asaurus. *¡Vamos!*"

2

Sunrise at 40,000 Feet

"Good morning, ladies and gentlemen. This is your captain speaking. Air traffic control has cleared us for departure on this nonstop flight to Mexico City. Weather looks good, and we don't anticipate any turbulence. We'll lose an hour to the time zone, so we should arrive in the capital city at about 8:30 local time. Please sit back, relax, and enjoy the ride."

Sage reached into the seat pocket in front of her and retrieved an airline magazine. She fanned through several articles and advertisements; all of them were dual language, with English text accompanied by Spanish. "Look, Izzy." She pointed to an article. "It's in both languages."

"Cool! This will help with your Spanish. We can practice during the flight."

The plane's interior lights dimmed, and Sage

poked Isabel's arm, then pointed out the window. The empty darkness outside was giving way to a hint of daylight, and she saw a couple of flashing lights on the plane's wing.

"I think we're taking off," she whispered to Isabel.

Sage felt her body pressing against the seat, and as the plane accelerated, she gripped both hand rests and stared at the trail of runway lights racing past her window. As she gazed into the dark sky, she felt a strange sensation; the bumpy runway suddenly smoothed out. She returned her attention to the ground and saw the runway's lights falling away from her window.

"Izzy, are we flying?" Sage spun her head around the cabin to see if anyone was as excited as she was. Except for Isabel, no one appeared to be.

"*¡Sí, amiga!*" Isabel said. "*¡Estamos voltando!*"

Aunt Drusilla poked a hand through the seats. "We're on our way now."

"And are you feeling okay, Aunt Dru?" Sage asked, thinking of Drusilla's health issues. Just last week, she was present when Aunt Dru fainted during the Smithsonian's award ceremony honoring her lifetime achievement in physics. That's when Sage learned that Drusilla's cancer had returned. And this time, it was in her blood.

"I feel great, Bird. Just relax."

For as long as Sage could remember, Drusilla had referred to her as 'Bird.' Legend had it that Sage was a scrawny newborn—"skin and bones" as Aunt Dru would say—and whenever Sage was hungry, she'd tilt her head back and chirp like a helpless baby bird. Drusilla joked that she never could tell whether baby Sage wanted a bottle of milk ... or a worm. Sage had always loved the nickname because it was something special she shared only with her Aunt Drusilla.

Suddenly Isabel pointed out the window. "Look at the clouds below!"

Sage glanced at the horizon then spun around. "Aunt Dru, are we in outer space?"

"Not quite, Bird. We *are* several miles above earth, but still safely within the atmosphere."

"How many miles?"

The cabin speaker hissed. "Good morning, everyone," a voice said. *"Buenos dias a todos.* Your captain here. We've reached our cruising altitude, and you may now use electronic devices. And aren't you all lucky this morning. Kindly turn your attention to the starboard side of the aircraft, and you'll have a front row seat to one of nature's most spectacular events—a sunrise at 40,000 feet."

As instructed, Sage gazed out the window. The brilliant pinks and yellows rising over the horizon were more vibrant that anything she'd ever seen.

This is too beautiful, she thought. *It's just too much.*

"Forty thousand feet," Aunt Dru said. "Tell me, how many miles is that?"

Sage loved a good math puzzle! She tapped Isabel on the arm. "Izzy, quick ... how many feet are in a mile? There are five thousand ... two hundred and ... two hundred and—"

Isabel didn't hesitate. "Five thousand, two hundred and eighty."

"You sure?"

Isabel tilted her head. "Is the atomic number of carbon six?"

Sage began drawing large numbers in the air as she calculated an answer. "So that's forty thousand divided by five-two-eight-zero. Let's see ... that equals ..."

"Holy cow!" Isabel said, leaning over Sage for another peek out the window. "Are you telling me we're seven and a half miles above the Earth?"

"No way!" Sage also glued her face to the window. "Look, Izzy!" Shards of sunlight pierced the clouds below and drenched the airplane cabin.

Isabel rested her head on Sage's shoulder and returned the in-flight magazine to the seat back ahead. The morning sun's sharp rays illuminated a small metal square on the plastic tray folded against the seat back. The metal square was about the size of a stick of chewing gum. Sage ran a finger over the smooth metal's surface and felt a rough texture in its middle. She looked closer and noticed a series of words engraved in the metal.

"Hmmm, that's interesting."

"What's interesting, Sage-asaurus?"

Sage noticed Isabel's eyes were closed. "This little metal sign. I was looking at it during our take-off, but I didn't even see these words etched into it. Well, not until the captain turned off the overhead lights, and the sun shined into the plane."

Isabel pried an eye open for a glimpse at what Sage was talking about. "That's easy, Sage-asaurus. Raking light."

"Raking light?"

"Well, it's actually *oblique* light, if you want to be exact. I picked that one up in Ms. Koonce's art class. When we were studying the post-impressionists." She yawned and closed her eyes again. "On our field trip to the National Gallery of Art, Ms. K wanted us to see every brushstroke, so she brought a flashlight to the museum. Then she stood next to each work of art and shined her light parallel across the canvas. That way, we could see every detail of the paint's texture."

"Raking light," Sage repeated.

"Sort of like how you can see dust particles in the air when the sun shines through your bedroom window at sunset. It's the sharp angle." Another yawn. "Lots of details in oblique light that would otherwise be invisible ..."

"Oblique light. Wow." She ran her finger over the metal plate again. "That's so cool, Izzy! Hey, do you wanna go back to the National Gallery of Art when we get home? You can show me Ms. K's flashlight trick up close ..."

She looked at Isabel again to find her already asleep, and covered her with a blanket. *Maybe I'll rest my eyes for a few minutes, too; then I'll watch the sun rise some more.* She placed her head against Isabel's. "Mexico, here we come. Frida, here we ..."

As she dozed off, Sage thought she heard her mother's voice. "Hey, Drusilla, I've got one for you. If you're American in the kitchen and you're Australian in the living room, then what are you in the ..."

3

The Miracle Hotel

"This is the last one," Mr. Carrington said. He retrieved a suitcase from the revolving carousel and hoisted it atop the mountain of bags balanced on a rolling cart. "Let's get to the street level. The hotel van should be waiting."

Sage followed her dad as the group exited the terminal, and the airport's cold, filtered air surrendered to Mexico's summer heat. *My first time outside the United States*, she thought. *I'm actually here. I'm in Mexico!* On arriving at the shuttle, she was overwhelmed by an endless line of taxis parked curbside. An orchestra of car horns, whistles, and shouting filled the morning air. *"Taxi, señora, señor. ¡Taxi aquí!"*

"Let's go, kids," Mrs. Flores said, sliding the shuttle's door open. "Hop in."

Sage examined several words printed on the van.

"*Hotel Milagro* ... the Miracle Hotel. Sounds great to me!" She walked to the rear of the shuttle and saw the driver loading their luggage in the back.

"*¡Hola, chula!*" the man said. "How are you today?"

"*Estoy muy bien, señor. ¡Gracias!*"

"*¿Hablas español, mi niña?*"

"*Bueno, un poco.* I'm trying to learn. I mean ... *¡estoy tentando de aprender!*" She lifted a small bag from the pile and stacked it neatly beside the others. "My friend, Isabel, is teaching me."

"*Que bien, chula.* You can sit inside. I take care of these bags for you. *Puedo hacerlo.*"

But Sage wanted to help him. "It's no problem. *No hay problema. Quiero ayudarte.*"

The man smiled. "*Muchas gracias, mi amiga.*"

"Sage?" Mrs. Carrington's head swiveled in search of her daughter. "Where's Sage?"

"I'm right here, Mommy."

Mrs. Carrington spun around. "What are you doing back there? Come sit inside the van." She exhaled. "Wandering around like that ... scared me half to death!"

Sage loaded one final bag into the shuttle. "*Bueno,* I should grab a seat. *Un placer conocerle, señor.*"

"The pleasure is all mine." He extended a hand. "*Soy Manuel.*"

She shook his hand. *"Mi nombre es Sage."*

"Mucho gusto, Sage."

"Mucho gusto."

She hopped around the shuttle and leapt inside, landing on top of Benji.

"Hey!" Benji said, adjusting his thick, red-rimmed glasses. "Watch it!"

"Nefertari Sage Carrington," her mom said. "Have a seat. And relax."

Sage squeezed in and closed the door.

"Looks like we're only about five miles from the Zocalo," Mr. Carrington said, examining a map.

"What's Zocalo?" Benji asked.

Manuel closed the luggage compartment, then opened the driver-side door.

"It's a large plaza in the middle of Mexico City," Mrs. Flores said. *"El Zócalo* is where the National Palace and the Angel of Independence are located."

"¿El Zócalo?" Manuel said. *"La Plaza de la Constitución. Es bonita.* Very beautiful."

"Shouldn't take us long to get there," Mr. Carrington said. "It's only a few miles down the highway, right?"

Manuel shrugged. *"Sí* ... and *no.* Yes, it is only seven kilometers from here. *Pero* ... well, you will see. The traffic here in *Distrito Federal es* ... very bad. Many people. And many cars. *Entonces,* we may take more time than one would expect." He checked his mirrors, then adjusted the air-conditioning vents. "*¿Cómo es la temperatura?* Does everyone receive the cold air?"

"Feels great!"

"Perfect!"

"Kids, do you all have your seat belts on?" Mrs. Flores asked. "Buckle up, please."

Click.

Click.

Click.

"*Entonces,*" Manuel said. "Let us go to Hotel Milagro!"

The shuttle pulled away from the curb, and Sage looked back at the terminal. The line of taxis remained as she shifted her attention to a magnificent sign resting atop the building: *Aeropuerto Internacional Benito Juárez.*

"Okay, my friends," Manuel said. "*Bienvenidos a la Ciudad de México.* Welcome to Mexico City! *Ahora*, you are in the largest city in the Americas, and one of the largest cities in the world." He weaved across several lanes of traffic. "*Aquí en la ciudad,* we have more museums than any other city … more than 160! And as you may know, we have twenty million *personas.*"

"Twenty million!?" Sage said.

"*Sí, amiga.*"

"Bruce," Sage's mom said, "how many people

live in Washington, DC?"

"Oh, well not even a million," he responded.

"Wow!" Sage said. "And there are *twenty* million here in Mexico City?!"

"*Es verdad*," Manuel said. "Twenty million people with six million cars."

"*Mucho trafico*," Isabel said as the van screeched to a halt.

"Everyone is okay?" Manuel asked.

"This is why we wear our seat belts," Mr. Carrington said in Sage's direction.

Just then, a siren blared behind the shuttle. The piercing sound grew louder as an ambulance approached.

"Oh no," Manuel said.

The ambulance inched through the gridlock before finally breaking free and driving past. In the wake of the emergency vehicle, a line of motorbikes roared down the cleared path.

Sage's eyes followed the bikes until—

Knock, knock, knock.

Outside the window, a vendor was rapping on the glass to get their attention. The man held several water bottles in one hand and small bags of snacks in the other. "*¡Agua fria!*" he shouted. "*¡Agua fria aquí!*"

"Because of all the traffic," Manuel said, "we have an industry in the street for sale of food and drinks." He chuckled to himself, then shifted the vehicle into park. *"Gracias a Dios* on days such as this one, because my friends, we may remain here for some time." He pointed ahead. "The ambulance *ésta allá. Un acidente."*

Now a woman strolled in front of the van. She balanced a woven basket atop her head. *"¡Tamales!"* she announced. *"Tengo tamales frescos."*

"Fresh tamales," Sage said. "Mmmm, *que delicioso* ... Mommy—"

Mrs. Carrington already knew Sage's next words. "Not now. Not here. We'll eat as soon as we get to the hotel, Sage."

"But, that could be forever."

"How long, do you think?" Mrs. Carrington asked Manuel.

"An hour," he responded. *"Más o menos."*

Mrs. Carrington's jaw dropped. "An hour!"

"But we're only three miles away," Mr. Carrington said.

"I have an idea," Benji said. "Our luggage has wheels, so we could just walk to the hotel."

"It is not safe, my friend." Manuel pointed ahead, to the site of the accident. "Cars on the road go very fast. We are most secure inside this van."

Sage noticed her mom scanning the vendors along the highway, then ...

Gurgle. Growl.

"Mommy," Sage said. "Was that you?"

Mr. Carrington touched his wife's stomach. "Sounds like someone's hungry."

The shuttle erupted with laughter.

"Don't worry, Lorraine," Drusilla said. "I'm right there with you."

"Me too," Mr. Flores added.

"Yeah."

"Yep."

"Same here."

Knock. Knock. Knock. Another vendor with baskets full of refreshments stood at Manuel's window, and he laughed. "Well, my friends. Would you like to make a buy for food and water?"

Gurgle. Growl. Mrs. Carrington wrapped both arms around her stomach. "I don't know if we should. I mean ... is it safe? The water ... can we drink it?"

Manuel examined a bottle. "It is high quality, *señora*. Very safe to drink for all visitors. Have no worry."

"Well ... okay then ... let's eat."

"Yes!" Sage said. "Tamales for me!"

"And two for me, please."

"Same here."

"I'll have one!"

The vendor shoveled food into the van as Sage gazed through the windshield at the endless sea of cars ahead.

"Here, babe." Mr. Carrington handed a small foil-covered package to Sage. "Careful, it's hot."

"*Caliente,*" Isabel said. "*Cuidado.*"

"And a water," Mr. Carrington handed a cold bottle to Sage.

"*Buen provecho,*" Manuel said.

Sage froze. "*¿Buen provecho?*"

"*Sí, chula.*"

"It's what we say before eating," Isabel said. "It means 'good health.'"

"That's so cool!" Benji said. "*Buen provecho,* everybody."

"*¡Buen provecho!*"

"*¡Buen provecho, Manuel!*"

"*¡Buen provecho, mis amigos!*"

Car horns and sirens filled the air as the group enjoyed their first meal together in Mexico City.

4

Beatriz the Angel

The shuttle turned onto a gravel driveway. Lush plants and trees flanked the sides of a red stone building with four large columns on its porch. A pair of hammocks was draped between the columns, and ceiling fans twirled above. As the van arrived, Sage noticed a young woman waving on the porch.

"*Es mi hija*," Manuel said. "My daughter, Beatriz." He looked at Sage and Isabel. "She is tour guide for you."

"How old is she?" Mrs. Carrington asked.

"Beatriz has eighteen years. And she is guide with *una licencia oficial* from the government of Mexico. Come. I present *mi hija* to you now." He honked the horn as the van came to a stop in front of the hotel. "My friends, welcome to the Miracle Hotel of *Distrito Federal*. You are guests, so please go inside and find comfort."

Sage flung the door open and hopped out. The afternoon sun kissed her arms, legs, and face as she tilted her head back, inhaled deeply, and filled her lungs with Mexico City.

"*¡Hola, bienvenidos a México!*" Beatriz greeted Sage and delivered a hug. "*Cómo estas? Mi nombre es Beatriz Gonzalez Padilla Montero.*"

She's beautiful! Sage thought looking at the slender young woman. Beatriz's curly brown hair fell below her shoulders, and several threads of yellow and pink string were woven into her locks. Her golden skin had been nourished by the vibrant Mexican sun, and Sage couldn't remember a time when someone's eyes seemed so full of life. "*¡Hola, Beatriz! Me llamo Sage Carrington. ¡Mucho gusto!*"

"*Mucho gusto, Sage. ¡Hablas español muy bien!*"

"Beatriz," Manuel said from the van. "*Por favor, mi amor,* speak English to our American friends!"

"*Sí, papa.* Yes, Father." Beatriz laughed, then returned her attention to Sage. "You speak Spanish very well."

Isabel trotted around the van and joined Sage. "Hi, Beatriz! I'm Isabel!"

"A pleasure to meet you."

"But I sometimes call her Izzy-dactyl," Sage said.

"Yeah, and I sometimes call *her* Sage-asaurus."

Beatriz chuckled. "*¿Por que?*"

"Well," Isabel said, "we kind of love dinosaurs."

"Yeah, they're awesome!" Sage added.

"That's why we have dinosaur nicknames." Isabel suddenly realized how weird she sounded. "Silly, huh?"

"*¡Que super!*" Beatriz shouted. "We are to become good friends. And I show you a very special side of my country. Sage, Isabel ... you are going to *love* Mexico."

Benji emerged from the van with a yawn, rubbing both of his eyes. "Are we there yet?" He scooted up to Isabel while putting on his glasses. "Is this the hotel—"

He froze at the sight of Beatriz.

"*Sí, amigo,*" Beatriz said. "You arrive."

Benji stood motionless, gazing at the woman.

She extended a hand. "I am Beatriz. It is a pleasure to know you."

Sage noticed Benji's silence and strange facial expression. She nudged him on the arm. "Hey ... Benji-raptor?" She waved a hand in front of his face. "Earth to Benji."

"Perhaps you are tired, my friend," Beatriz said as Benji's face eased into a soft smile. "Please enter the hotel and locate a chair. Rest for a time."

Drusilla led Benji up the porch and into the hotel. The goofy smile stayed on his face, and his eyes remained fixed on Beatriz the entire time.

"Is your friend okay?" Beatriz asked. "He is able to talk?"

Isabel shook her head in disbelief. "Anybody else on the planet right now would be asking us, 'Does he ever shut up?'"

"Benji's *never* that quiet."

"Hmmm, *que interestante*," Beatriz said. "Perhaps he is fatigued."

"Eleven year olds," Sage said, rolling her eyes.

Beatriz led the girls up the front steps. "And how old are you?"

Isabel wrapped her arm around Sage's shoulders. "We're *twelve*."

"Well, almost thirteen. Izzy's birthday is tomorrow."

"And Sage-asaurus turns thirteen next week."

"*¡Feliz cumpleanos para ustedes! Geminis,*" Beatriz said.

"*Gracias,*" Isabel said. "Yep, both Geminis!"

"You girls have much luck to travel the world at young ages. I think about words from *San Augustin*, 'The world is a book, and those who do not travel read only a page.'"

"I love that!" Sage said.

"Double love! And when's your birthday, Beatriz?"

"*Diciembre.*"

"December," Isabel said. "So you're a ..."

"*Sagitario.*"

"Sagittarius. Cool!"

"You are young women now."

Sage felt uneasy at the thought of adulthood, although she couldn't figure out exactly why. "Yeah, I guess so."

"Do you wish to enter the hotel and to relax for a time?"

Sage looked at Isabel; neither was excited about that option.

"No? Hmmm, well we have other selections. There is always—"

Both girls chimed in, "We want to see Frida Kahlo's museum!"

Beatriz fell back a bit from the unexpected announcement. "I see. Well, *claro*, we can visit *el museo*. Do you like Frida?"

"We *love* her!"

Beatriz nodded. "She was an amazing woman, no? A true *mexicana*. As a country, we are quite proud of her story. *Entonces*, we go to the *museo*."

"Yes!" Sage high-fived Isabel.

"Your bags are inside the hotel. I go talk to your parents, and discover if others would like to travel with us. *¿Ésta bien?*"

"*¡Bien!*"

"Sure!"

"*Bueno.*" Beatriz extended a hand to each girl.

33

"*Vamos, amores.*" Sage clutched one hand and Isabel grabbed the other as the trio entered the hotel together. "Let us go and see Frida!"

5

The Blue House

Life-sized plaster skeletons guarded the entrance of a blue concrete building. Resting above its green front door, a sign constructed of tiny ceramic squares welcomed all visitors: *Museo Frida Kahlo*.

Beatriz opened her arms and announced, "*Bienvenidos a la casa de Frida.* Come with me."

The girls locked arms as they followed Beatriz and Benji into a lush interior garden. Tropical plants and pre-Columbian pottery decorated the courtyard, and a miniature pyramid rested at the end of the walkway. "Izzy, look! A pyramid!" The girls jogged across the courtyard, and Sage observed a beautiful collection of statues and pottery atop the structure.

Beatriz caught up to the girls. "This was an idea of Diego."

"Her husband, Diego Rivera?" Sage asked.

"*Eso*. He wanted to show respect for the great builders of Mexico. And as you see, this construction also shows a magnificent collection of pre-Hispanic artifacts."

"Sage!" Isabel pointed across the courtyard, then sprinted to a blue concrete wall. She traced her fingers along several words scrawled in white paint: *Frida y Diego vivieron en ésta casa 1929–1954.*

Sage and Benji jogged over.

"Can you read it?" Benji asked.

Sage tilted her head. "It says, 'Frida and Diego ... live in this house.'"

"*Lived*," Isabel said. "Past tense, Sage-asaurus. *Vivieron.*"

"Frida and Diego *lived*." Sage touched the wall and imagined Frida's skilled hands painting the message decades earlier.

Isabel shook Sage's arm. "*She* lived here!"

"It is true," Beatriz said. "Frida Kahlo and Diego Rivera shared this house for many years as a married couple. Frida made great paintings here."

"Inside this house?"

Beatriz nodded. "Much of her art remains today. Would you like to see?"

"Yes!"

"Absolutely!"

Benji yawned. He didn't seem amused. "Let's get it over with already." He motioned to Sage and

Isabel. "It's all they've been talking about since forever. 'Frida this' and 'Frida that.' It's enough to wear a kid out, ya know?"

"You could've just stayed at the hotel, Benji!"

Isabel lowered her camera. "Yeah, Benji-raptor. Why'd you even come out if you weren't interested in seeing the museum?"

Sage caught Benji staring at Beatriz as she entered the house. "Ah, okay, *now* I know why Benji wanted to come with us."

"Of course!" Isabel tapped her camera. "Hey, Benji, you want me to take a picture of you two love birds?"

"Benji and Beatriz."

"B and B!"

"That's not funny, Sage. Stop, Izzy! I just … I wanna see the museum! That's all. Promise!"

"Benjamin!" Beatriz called from inside the house. "Come, *mi amor*. Let us see the paintings."

Sage and Isabel leaned against each other. "Oohhh … *'mi amorrrr!'*"

"It's just an expression! You know," Benji cleaned his glasses with his shirt, "for a couple of twelve year olds, you guys can be *so* immature sometimes." He replaced his glasses, raised his chin, and strutted inside the house.

"Well, excuuuuse us!" Sage turned to Isabel. "Ready, *mi amor*?"

"Yes, *mi amor*."

They imitated Benji by straightening their clothes and raising their chins, and then strutted inside to the sound of each other's giggles.

The playful energy melted away, and Sage's heart filled with anticipation as she crossed the threshold into Frida's home. She had imagined this moment a thousand times. *And now we're actually here*, she thought. *We're inside the Blue House!* She wiped a sweaty palm against her shorts, then grabbed Isabel's hand.

"Frida Kahlo was born in this house," Beatriz said. "She learned to paint here, and forty-seven years after her birth, she also died here."

"Can I take pictures?" Isabel asked.

"Yes, of course," Beatriz responded. "But when we are inside of the *museo*, photography without flash, please."

Framed paintings decorated all four walls. Sage's eyes wandered across the room while Isabel began snapping pictures. As she examined the portraits, she noticed that none of the faces were of Frida.

"These early paintings are of friends and family. You see her sister—Cristina. You also see *Portrait of a Girl*. Oh, and here is a collection of native Indian women. Frida possessed extraordinary gifts to see beyond the surface. Then, we have our first self-portraits."

"How many did she paint?"

"Seventy self-portraits, Isabel. *Más o menos*."

"She was so beautiful!"

"*Atlética*, too," Beatriz said. "As a girl, she competed in swimming, boxing, and wrestling. You must remember, at this moment in the history of Mexico, activities such as these were quite uncommon for a girl."

"Frida was unique," Sage said.

"In every way." Beatriz strolled across the room. "In her childhood, Frida would spend much time with her father. She adored him. Guillermo Kahlo was a professional photographer—"

"Just like Izzy!"

Isabel lowered her camera. "I wouldn't say I'm a *professional*, Sage-asaurus!" She smirked. "Well, not *yet*, anyway."

"Frida often traveled with her father on photography assignments. It is at this point in her life that she learned about color, composition, shadow, and light. Guillermo taught her the properties of light, which she would use to become a great painter."

Sage pointed to a note displayed under a glass case. "Izzy!" She examined the handwritten message. "It's in English!" She scratched her head. "But I thought Frida spoke Spanish?"

"When she was slightly older than you—at fifteen years—she attended the finest school in Mexico

City where she learned *three* different languages. Frida Kahlo was of a brilliant mind."

"Three languages!?" Sage shook her head. "I only know *one*! Well, I'm *trying* to learn Spanish, but … wow, three!"

Beatriz nodded. "*Claro*, Sage. Frida spoke in English. She was, how do you say, *fluente*?"

"Fluent?"

"*Eso*. Many people do not know of this fact. But Frida spent much time in America. Four years with Diego. They stayed for a time in San Francisco, Detroit, and New York City."

"Such an amazing life." Sage returned her attention to the note and read several lines aloud. "'Revolution is the harmony of form and color, and everything exists and moves under only one law: life. Nobody is separate from anybody else. Nobody fights for himself. Everything is all and one. Anguish and pain, pleasure and death, are no more than a process for existence. I paint a little bit. Not because I consider myself an artist. Rather, I offer my creative gifts, for I am a soldadera of the revolution. My beloved Mexico was born in the year 1910, as was I.'"

"Wow, she was born more than 100 years ago."

"It is true, Benjamin."

"1910?" Isabel said. "But that's *not* when Frida was born."

Beatriz shrugged. "Well, yes and no. Many who study her life believe Frida was born earlier, perhaps in the year 1907. *Pero*, when she grew older, she many times told of a birth in the year 1910. This is of special significance in the history of Mexico. It is the year of our country's revolution."

Sage unzipped Isabel's backpack and retrieved the *Book of Love*. She flipped the pages, grabbed a pen, and began jotting notes. "What does Frida mean by *soldadera*?"

"Good question, Sage. *Soldaderas* were the women soldiers of the Mexican Revolution."

Sage scribbled several notes. "You mean ... women actually *fought*?"

"*Sí*," Beatriz said. "During the time of my country's revolt, many women entered into the conflict. Mothers, sisters, and wives stood beside the Mexican men. Some provided food and medical help. Others fought ... and died."

Benji adjusted his glasses. "I never heard of the soldaderas before."

"Me neither," Isabel added.

Beatriz smiled. "This is from where I receive my name."

Sage stopped writing. "Beatriz?"

"I have the name of a great *soldadera*, Beatriz Gonzales Ortega," she said.

"You have a pretty name," Benji said with an

impossible grin.

Beatriz winked at him. *"Gracias, mi amor."*

Sage and Isabel snickered loud enough to catch Benji's attention, and he rolled his eyes.

"Can you tell us more about Beatriz Ortega?" he asked.

"Claro. In the time of our revolution, Señora Ortega saved many lives with her knowledge of science and medicine. As a nurse, she helped *all* wounded soldiers, for it did not matter on which side of the battle they fought. To this day in Mexico, her name is a *representación* of peace, kindness, and integrity." Beatriz kissed a finger, then made the sign of the cross, running from her forehead to her torso and shoulders. "She is forever an angel of the revolution."

Sage continued jotting. "Incredible."

"So Frida was also a soldadera in the war?" Isabel asked.

"Couldn't have been." Sage ran some numbers in her head. "She would've only been a baby."

"You are correct, Sage. In truth, she was a young child during the revolution. But Frida says she and Mexico were given life in the same year. This is a popular story Frida wants you to believe. *En realidad*, she was birthed in the year 1907." Beatriz returned her attention to the glass case. "With this letter, perhaps Frida wants to say that in her heart, she was a *soldadera*."

Sage wrote furiously in the journal. "I think it's cool that she changed her birthday to match the revolution!"

"Frida Kahlo is a woman of great mystery. And one of the most *inteligente* in the history of Mexico. The word for this, I learned—when I was in school for English—Frida is an enigma."

"E-nig-ma," Sage said, while scribbling.

Click. Click. Isabel captured more shots of the letter before advancing to a large portrait on the wall.

Sage tilted her head to the ceiling for a better look.

"This portrait is called *The Broken Column,*" Beatriz said. "She painted it in the year 1944. It reflects a great tragedy in her early life. We can see into her body in this picture. The backbone is displayed as a broken concrete column. Notice the nails piercing her skin and the tears flowing from her eyes."

"What's wrapped around her body?" Benji asked.

"It is a medical corset," Beatriz said. "A metal brace around the torso for support, Benjamin. Due to the horrific accident of her early years."

Frida's stern gaze leapt from the painting and shook Sage's spirit. The shattered bones inside Frida's body contrasted with the remarkable strength in her posture and facial expression. *How could she have survived so much pain?*

"What accident?" Benji asked.

"It was quite an unexpected event in her life," Beatriz said.

Sage continued examining Frida's broken body as she quietly said, "The bus."

"*Eso.*" Beatriz exhaled deeply before telling the story. "When Frida had eighteen years, she was injured quite seriously. A wooden bus carrying her collided with a streetcar. On that day, she suffered on the street with a spine and pelvis broken in three places, and a right leg broken in eleven places. Her collarbone and three ribs were shattered, her right foot was dislocated and crushed. Finally, a metal pole from the trolley remained inside her body. The pole entered here." Beatriz pointed to her arm-pit, motioned across her chest and stomach, and stopped at the top of her thigh. "The pole exited here, through ... how do you say ... her birth canal."

"How awful!"

"It is a miracle she survived," Beatriz said.

"Thank goodness."

"During the period of recovery, Frida's father brought her a set of brushes and paint. This is when she first began to paint."

Sage spotted a small panel below the painting and read the quote inscribed, "'Not more than a few days ago, I was a child who went about in a world of colors. Now I live in a painful planet, transparent as ice. I became old in an instant. You cannot imagine the hopelessness one comes to feel. I paint myself because I am so often alone, and I am the subject I know best ... Frida Kahlo.'"

"So much pain," Isabel said.

"If this were not enough," Beatriz said, "for her remaining life, she was saddened by a hardship of not bearing children. She possessed a full heart with much love to give. And with great desire, she wanted to make a family with Diego."

"So ... did they ever have children?" Benji asked.

"She was pregnant three times, but lost all of ..." Beatriz seemed overcome with emotion. "In life, *mis amigos*, we do not always receive what it is that we want." She proceeded farther into the home.

Sage thought she heard Beatriz sniffle. "Is she okay, Izzy?"

Isabel exhaled; she also seemed moved by the emotional moment. "Are *you*?"

Sage took Isabel's hand as they advanced to the next room.

An easel rested in the middle of a window-filled room. An antique wheelchair faced the easel and containers of paintbrushes and charcoal pens decorated a nearby table.

"This is Frida's studio," Beatriz announced. "You

can see her space was quite large."

"She sat here and painted?" Sage asked, while Isabel photographed the room.

"*Sí*." Beatriz pointed to the wheelchair. "In this seat."

Sage examined the flimsy wheels and wooden frame of the antique chair. Beside the easel, a window overlooked the sun-drenched courtyard.

"And through here, we will find Frida's bedroom." Beatriz led the kids through another doorway.

A four-poster bed rested on one side of the room, and a mirror decorated the ceiling directly above the bed. One of Frida's traditional Tehuana outfits adorned a mannequin in the corner; the floral headpiece, square-cut blouse, and hand-stitched skirt demonstrated immaculate attention to detail. On the floor beside the mannequin was a small footstool with the word 'Frida' painted across its front.

"Clothing, jewelry, shoes, and styles of hair were important pieces of her identity," Beatriz said. "She was a traditional *mexicana*, and at the same time, an individual."

"An enigma," Sage whispered.

Click. Click. Isabel captured the footstool, then lowered her camera. "Sage, here it is!" She tiptoed closer to the wall.

"Here *what* is?" Benji asked.

Both girls responded, "*The Two Fridas!*"

Sage stood motionless, mouth agape, staring at a mural as Beatriz described the scene. "Perhaps this is her most *famosa* painting. From the year 1939. It is called *The Two Fridas*. They sit side by side, holding hands. The Frida on the right is the loved Frida. We know this because she wears traditional *mexicana* clothes and her skin is dark, healthy. She has a full heart and holds a tiny portrait of Diego. It is from this portrait which blood—life—flows. Unloved Frida on the left wears a sterile white dress. The lace of her clothing is torn, and we see an incomplete heart. In her hand, a surgical instrument stops the flow of blood from the heart."

Sage leaned in for a closer examination. "Look at her brushstrokes. The detail is amazing."

"Yeah," Isabel said. "Textures. Composition. Even the way she used shadows and highlights."

Sage continued examining the fine details of each stroke. "A true artist."

Beatriz sniffled again. "Excuse me please, *amigas*. I will await you outside. Take your time, and come when you are prepared."

Sage motioned to Beatriz. "Was she crying?"

"Maybe she loves Frida more than we do." Isabel changed the film in her camera, then resumed photographing the portrait. "A few more photos and we'll go and check on her."

"Okay, Izzy." Sage returned her attention to

the mural. "We're here. It's here. *She's* here." She looked at Isabel. Her friend's glassy eyes barely contained the tears, and one finally escaped and ran down her cheek. Sage felt tears filling her own eyes, but then noticed the dress hems of the Fridas in the painting. *Are those…no, couldn't be. Must be my tears.* Isabel took several photos as Sage wiped her eyes and reexamined the stitching of the clothes; sure enough, a tiny stream of numbers, fractions, decimals, and shapes marched across the bottom of Frida's dresses.

"Square, 0.75, 2/3, 9, 0.67, 1/5 … no way! Pentagon, 2/8, pentagon, 10/30, 0.5." She nodded. "It is. It *really* is!"

Isabel heard Sage's excitement. "What? What is it?"

"The stitching, Izzy. Look at the hems."

Isabel leaned in, then whispered, "Heart, 0, 8, 10/20, 1/5, 1/2 …" She looked at Sage. "Is this what I think it is? No way. *Can't* be."

"It *can!*"

Isabel stepped back. "Are you telling me that Frida painted a…a–"

"Cryptogram!"

6

Frida's Secret

"A secret message?" Benji said. "Get outta here! Inside *The Two Fridas*!?"

"Shhh!" Sage said as a couple of museum visitors passed behind them. "Izzy, did you get pictures of their dresses?"

"Let me grab a few more with my macro lens."

"Make sure you photograph the whole thing." She scanned the room to see if anyone might have overheard their discovery. It didn't appear so. As she reexamined the symbols painted on the dresses, she also observed a string of shallow grooves etched into the canvas. The grooves were only visible when she viewed the painting at a sharp angle; they reminded her of turning to a fresh sheet in her notebook and seeing pen marks pressed through from the previous page.

Click. Click. Click. Click.

Sage looked at the mural once more; this time her attention was on the facial expressions of the two Fridas. Their stern looks seemed to hide deep thoughts *and, perhaps,* she thought, *an amazing secret.*

Isabel continued photographing the scene. "Any idea what kind of cryptogram it is, Sage-asaurus?"

Sage opened the *Book of Love* and began copying the code. "Looks like classic substitution, Izzy. But who knows, with all these fractions and decimals, it could be more difficult ... maybe polyalphabetic."

"Well, there's only one way to find out."

"I'll copy the whole message by hand, so we'll have a backup for your photos."

"Good idea. You never know when we might need a second copy."

Sage smiled at her. "Always be prepared, right?"

Benji looked over Sage's shoulder as she continued jotting. "I wonder what it says."

"Zero, 0.33, square, hexagon, 0.75, 1/3, 0.2, 2/3, parallelogram ... Don't know, Benji-raptor. But we're going to find out."

"We can decipher Frida's message tonight," Isabel said. "When we get back to the hotel."

"Triangle, 0.67, star, 2/3, 8, 1/4, 1/3. Okay," Sage mumbled to herself. "I think that's the whole cipher."

At that moment, Beatriz poked her head inside.

"My friends, time has come to leave. *¿Estan listos?*"

Benji spun around. "Hey, Beatriz, guess what!"

Oh no! Sage thought. *Benji's going to tell her about the cryptogram!* She panicked and elbowed him.

"Ow!"

"You have a question, Benjamin?"

Sage could sense Benji's defenses crumbling to Beatriz's soft gaze. She tossed another elbow to snap him out of it.

"Hey, that hurt!"

She shook her head and shot him a look.

Benji received the message. "It's nothing, Beatriz." He rubbed his arm. "Yeah, we're ready."

"*Perfecto. ¡Vamos!*" Beatriz exited again.

"We have to solve this cryptogram alone, guys." Sage closed the journal and returned it to Isabel's bag. "Just us. *Without* the adults."

"But why?"

"Because it's our secret," Isabel said.

"Exactly."

"I don't know." Benji stepped back. "Maybe they can help us figure it out."

"Sage! Isabel! Benji!" Beatriz said from the courtyard. "The night is coming. We must return to the hotel."

"Let's solve it together," Sage said. "After dinner. Okay?" She extended a hand, and Isabel placed hers on top. "Come on, Benji-raptor."

Benji seemed apprehensive but finally stacked a hand on top of Isabel's. "Okay ... fine."

"¡*Vamos!*"

"Let's go!"

The kids raised their hands to the ceiling then dashed out of the house.

We're going to solve this cryptogram, Sage thought while trotting across the courtyard. *No doubt about it, Frida. We'll decipher your message. I promise!*

7

Bedtime Decryption

A flashlight beam danced along the walls, the only light in an otherwise dark room. Various paintings and cultural tapestries came to life as the light shone brightly on them. Outside the window, a moonless sky sparkled with oodles of twinkling stars.

Sage sat between Isabel and Benji on the floor, a large sheet of paper resting in front of them. The paper was full of decimals, fractions, integers, and geometric shapes.

"Our first night in Mexico!" Benji announced.

"Shhh!" Isabel pointed the flashlight at his face. "You'll wake up our parents."

"Ow!" He raised a hand to block the light. "My eyes!"

Sage leaned in. "Quiet, Benji!"

He pointed to Isabel, maintaining the same high

volume. "Then tell Isabel to quit shining that thing in my face!"

Both girls shoved him. "Quiet!"

"Guys," Sage said in a more serious tone, "the cryptogram! Let's get to work. We have to figure out what it all means." She examined the characters on the paper:

2/5 2/3 4 0.33 1/4 5 4/6 5 1/2 1/5

6/9 1/3 ♥ 0 8 10/20 1/5 1/2 ⬡ 3/9

0.25 1 0 0.40 1/3 15/25.

⬡ 4/12 ⬠ 2/8 ⬠ 10/30 0.5 0

1/2 0.2 6/10 2/3 4 1/2 0.6 0 4/8 0.5

3/5 4/12 6/9 2 1/5 2/3 3/5 △

1/2 9 2/3 0.2 1/2 4 △ △ 1/2 4

2/5 5 1 2/4 3/15 8/20

△ 1/3 △ 0.4 0.5 2 1/3.

0.5 0.6 3/6 4/16 9 8/12 0.25 2/3 0.75
8/20 10/30 0.6 0.67 0.75 2/5 1/3 6/10
2/3 5/20 △ 6/12 4/16 ▱ 0.33
0.75 2/3 0.25 1/3.

3 1 ☐ 0.75 2/3 9 0.67 1/5 4/6 4
6/15 15/20 5/15 15/25 1/3 6 0.33 ☐
12/18 3 0.4 50/100 10/50 0 0.33 ☐
⬡ 0.75 1/3 0.2 2/3 ▱ 7 0.5
9/15 5/15 △ 7/14 2/3 4 4/12 5/25.

☐ 2/5 0.6 3/4 6/12 1/5 2/3 4 1/2
3/5 0 1/2,
♡ 2/10 0.4 △ 0.67 ☆ 2/3 8
1/4 1/3

"You sure this ciphertext is correct?"

"I'm sure, Benji." Sage rotated the paper. "I copied every character exactly the way Frida wrote it in her painting."

"Too bad we can't double-check the cipher with my photos." Isabel lowered her head. "Sorry I couldn't develop them, guys." She rummaged through her backpack. "I just don't know what could have happened to my red light. The other supplies are here—film clips, thermometer, cartridge opener, chemical fixer—but without my safelight, I won't be able to process the film." She pointed to the ceiling. "These fluorescent lights would expose the negatives."

"It's okay, Izzy." Sage leaned closer to the paper. "We've got my notes from the *Book of Love*."

"I just hope we're not missing any details," Isabel said. "My macro lens picks up everything ... even stuff we can't see with our eyes."

"Don't sweat it." Sage grabbed a pen and made long dashes under each character in Frida's cipher. "I'll write the plaintext answer beneath each symbol in the cryptogram as we decipher it."

Isabel continued rifling through her backpack. "Well, just in case, my cousin, Victor, is also a photographer. And he lives in Veracruz. We'll be there tomorrow, so I'll use his darkroom to process all my negatives."

"Sounds like a plan, Izzy. But for now ..." Sage

finished writing the dashes. "Let's decrypt Frida's message!"

"We can figure out a missing letter here and there by using the other words and letters around it."

"Cipher context," Sage said.

"Exactly. Hey, I wonder if the message is in Spanish or English."

"Oh, that's right," Benji said. "Beatriz said Frida spoke three languages."

"Guys!" Sage pointed to the end of the code. "I think I already figured out the first piece. Look!" She spun the paper around. "The very last line of symbols." She tapped her finger along a series of characters. "Heart 2/10 0.4 triangle 0.67 ... then a big space and ... star 2/3 8 1/4 1/3."

"So?" Benji said. "It's just a bunch of fractions, shapes, and decimals."

"Look closer, Benji-raptor." Sage pointed to the code as Isabel and Benji leaned in. "The final two words of her note."

Isabel's face lit up. "A signature!" She snapped her fingers. "It's her name!"

"I think so." Sage rotated the *Book of Love* and wrote the encoded letters in a column on the page's margin. She then jotted Frida's full name next to the corresponding symbols: F-R-I-D-A K-A-H-L-O. "We can test my idea. Look, the letter 'A' appears in her first *and* last name. So it should be the same symbol in both places of the cipher."

♡ 2/10 0.4 △ 0.67 ☆ 2/3 8

1/4 1/3

Isabel tapped the paper while counting the characters. "F, R, I, D … so 0.67 should be the letter A."

Sage nodded. "That means we should see 0.67 again as the second letter of her last name—another A."

"Isabel continued counting. "Oh no! This symbol's different. It's 2/3."

"Aw, man," Sage said. "But I was *sure* this was her name!"

"Good guess, Sage-asaurus."

Benji tapped her on the shoulder. "Yeah, that was close."

That would have been so perfect, Sage thought. *Frida's name would have given us tons of letters to substitute into the cipher.*

"Two-tenths," Isabel repeated. "Two-thirds … wow, feels like we're back in Mrs. Gill's class, huh, with these fractions and decimals? All we need is for her to jump out and announce a pop quiz!

'Convert all fractions into decimal form, ladies and gents, and be sure to solve for two decimal places.'" Isabel shivered. "I don't want to think about school for our next ten weeks of vacation."

Wait a second! Sage thought, as she replayed Isabel's voice in her head. *Convert these fractions …*

"I *hate* pop quizzes!" Benji said. "Why can't teachers just tell us in advance so we can prepare—"

"Izzy!" Sage looked at the column of characters again. "That's it!"

"*What's* it?"

"Look." She scribbled 2/3 on the paper, followed by an equal sign and then 0.67.

"Holy cow!"

"What is it?" Benji said. "What!?"

"Benji! These two numbers … they're equivalent!"

"Equiva—what?"

"*Equivalent*, Benji-raptor. That means they're mathematically the same."

Isabel grabbed another pen and began writing across the paper. "Yeah, Benji, 2/3 is equal to 0.67 … and 1/2 equals 0.5 … and 1/3 equals 0.33. These are all equivalent *ratios*."

Sage dropped her pen in amazement. "Boy, Frida's good. She's using *different* fractions and decimals to represent the *same* letters. It's a *polynumeric* math cipher! She's playing with *equivalent ratios*."

Benji placed his chin on Sage's shoulder. "Are you sure?"

"Let's test it out," Sage said. "First, I'll fill in the letters in Frida's name, including those two A's."

Isabel scooted closer to Sage and Benji. "If this is correct, then we'll have a bunch of deciphered letters: F, R, I, D, K, H, L, and O!"

Sage filled in the blanks. "Yep! So we'd know the heart, 2/10, 0.4, triangle, star, 8, 1/4, and 1/3."

Isabel cheered quietly. "Let's see if we can figure out some more."

Sage stared at the remaining numbers and symbols on the page. *What does it all mean?* she wondered. *And which letters can we solve next? Think, Sage!*

"Seems strange," Benji said, rotating the paper for a better look.

Sage paused. "What seems strange?"

"That Frida would write this whole long letter and then just add her name at the bottom. Doesn't she have any manners?"

"What are you talking about, Benji?" Isabel slid the paper away from him and rotated it back.

"Just last month, at the end of the school year, I was working on my handwriting with Mr. Ray." He adjusted his glasses. "You know him? One of my favorite teachers. One time, he gave me a star just for coming to the board and spelling the words 'tidal wave.' It was awesome because all my class-mates thought it was T-I-T-L-E, and—"

"Benji, please!" Sage dropped her pen. "Get to the point!"

"Oh." He cleared his throat. "Well, I was going to, if you'd just quit rushing me! I was saying that Mr. Ray taught us how to write letters. You know, the proper way to format and all. So we learned about the opening—'Dear so and so'—then the body of the note. And finally ... ,the closing. That's where we write 'Sincerely,' and then finish with our signa-ture—"

Sage flinched. *Closing!* she thought. *A formal closing ... before the signature.*

Benji continued. "That's what I was saying with my handwriting. You know, cursive is really tough for me, but I'm trying to improve—"

"Benji, that's it!"

"What? My cursive?"

"Yes! I mean, no!" Sage picked up the pen. "Frida's cipher. Her closing." She looked at Isabel. "Izzy, how do you say 'sincerely' in Spanish?"

"Easy," Isabel said. "Any word ending in 'ly' changes to 'mente.' So 'sincerely' becomes *'sinceramente.'*"

Sage jotted down the symbols displayed before Frida's signature on the paper and began counting its letters.

"How many is it?" Isabel asked.

"Twelve," Sage said. "And *sinceramente* has ..."
"Twelve letters."

Benji slid over and sat shoulder to shoulder as they all looked closely:

◻ 2/5 0.6 3/4 6/12 1/5 2/3 4 1/2

3/5 0 1/2,

"We should already have some of the letters from her name, right?" Isabel scooted to the other side of Sage. "Such as the I, R, and A."

"You're right, Izzy. I'll substitute those three in and see what we get." She wrote the deciphered letters on the page:

◻ i 0.6 3/4 6/12 r a 4 1/2 3/5

0 1/2,

Benji leaned closer. "The I, R, and A look like they're in the right spots, don't they?"

Sage's heart skipped a beat. "Yes! They do!"

"But look!" Benji said. "The two E's at the end are both 1/2." He pointed to the symbol before the 'R'. "But here it's 6/12. That's not right, is it?"

Did we make a mistake? Sage wondered. *But I*

thought we already figured out Frida's pattern ... the decimals and fractions were equivalent. "Six-twelfths," she repeated. *What am I missing?*

"I've got it!"

"What do you see, Izzy-dactyl?"

"It's the same as before. Proportions! Six-twelfths and one-half. They're equivalent!"

"You're right!"

"So, we need to go through Frida's message and break all the fractions down to their lowest common denominators."

"Wow, Izzy, now you really *do* sound like Mrs. Gill!"

"That means we *are* on the right track." Isabel grabbed another pen and began writing. "And it means we get more deciphered letters! *Sinceramente*," she repeated to herself. "Now we have S, N, C, M, E, and T!"

"Let's fill them all in!"

"Kids!" Mrs. Flores' voice yelled through the wall. "Bedtime!"

Sage held a finger to her mouth. "Quiet, guys. We *have* to finish deciphering Frida's message before we go to bed!"

Sage continued calculating equivalent values and substituting the various plaintext letters into the blanks.

"We broke the code!" Sage said as her eyes

darted between the ciphertext and plaintext. "We're solving Frida's cipher. We almost have the whole thing."

Isabel tossed her arm around Sage. "So what does it say!?"

"Nefertari Sage Carrington!" Sage's mom shouted from another room.

"Okay, Mommy!" Sage returned her attention to Frida's message. "And this must be a D ... and these are all T's. Plus we already know anything equivalent to 3/4 is C. So the pentagon shape must be a V."

"I can still see the flashlight!" Sage's mom announced.

"Benji, cover the light with your hand!"

The kids huddled around the dimly-lit paper as Sage dropped the pen and exhaled deeply. They all leaned in to read the deciphered message:

I am soldadera of the revolution.

Yo vivo eternamente en la grande pared de mi querido diego.

En el palacio nacional del zocalo.

Busca para mi con ojos abiertos y corazon lleno de amor.

Sinceramente,

Frida Kahlo

"I am soldadera of the revolution." Benji pointed at the remaining message. "Isabel, what's the rest say?"

"'I am soldadera of the revolution ... I live eternally in the great wall of my dear Diego ... in the National Palace of the Zocalo ... Search for me with eyes open and a heart full of love ... Sincerely, Frida Kahlo.'"

In the faint light, Sage saw expressions of amazement on her friends' faces. "Can. You. Believe it!?"

They all buzzed with excitement.

"A message from Frida!"

"We deciphered it!"

"'Great wall of my dear Diego'," Sage repeated. "'National Palace ... search for me ... Zocalo.'"

"That's where we're going tomorrow," Isabel said. "With Beatriz. Maybe Frida left another clue there."

"Lights out!" Mrs. Carrington shouted. "Final warning, young lady!"

"Izzy, flashlight!" She clicked the light off.

Benji's glasses sparkled in the starlight. "Frida's gonna send us all over the place chasing her clues. I just *know* she is! And I'll tell you another thing ... we're not home in DC, where we can just go anywhere we want, anytime we want. Like the treasure hunt last week. Remember? We ran all over Washington tracking that map. The Museum of

Natural History. The National Mall—"

Sage tried to calm him down. "Benji ..."

"The memorials and the monuments—that was no sweat." He stood up. "But now we're in Mexico. And we have an *itinerary*! We should just give up. Besides, how can we decipher messages while we're traveling all over the country ... the pyramids, Cozumel, Veracruz, Chicken Itza." He shuffled to a small bed in the corner and plopped down. "I say let's just enjoy Mexico. Forget about the cryptogram."

But there was no way Sage could abandon secret messages from Frida Kahlo. "You don't have to help us, Benji." She shook her head. "And it's *Chichen* Itza. Not chicken."

"Whatever." He took his glasses off and climbed under the covers.

"Fine, Benji-raptor." Isabel folded the paper and stuffed it into her backpack. "Sage and I will solve it—alone."

"I don't care. Goodnight."

Sage knew Benji wouldn't be content as the odd man out. That was the thing with eleven year olds. They always wanted to be a part of the action, *especially* when the action involved twelve year olds. He'd come around.

"Goodnight, Benji-raptor." She climbed into bed and pulled the covers overhead—her preferred way to sleep. "Goodnight, Izzy-dactyl."

"*Buenas noches.*"

As the quiet Mexican night carried Sage to sleep, her thoughts remained on the cipher. *In the great wall. Diego. The Zocalo. National Palace. We'll investigate all of it tomorrow with Beatriz. Don't worry, Frida. We're gonna follow your clues as far as possible. But we only have three more days in Mexico, so try to not make it impossible for us. We'll do our best, okay? I promise we will ...*

8

Morning in Mexico

Familiar voices laughed in the distance.

"He didn't," Sage's mom said. "You're kidding!"

"Lorraine, I'm telling you," Drusilla said. "It's true!"

Sage heard the clamor of pots and pans and imagined the adults were in the kitchen, preparing breakfast. She caught a whiff of an unknown peppery aroma. It wasn't her familiar bacon or ham. *Sausage?* she thought. *Mmmm, maybe spicy sausage! Whatever it is ... smells delish!* Few culinary treats aroused her taste buds like spicy food. Her mom and dad didn't care for it, but she adored the hot stuff.

She pried one eye open to see the early-morning sun shining brightly through the window. She opened her other eye, and scanned the room. Benji's bed was empty; the only remnant from his snooze was a wrinkled pillow resting atop a neatly made-up bed. Isabel slept nearby in a cot. Sage looked at the calm expression on her best friend's face. She always loved how Isabel smiled softly while sleeping.

"Today," Sage said, "we're going to figure out what that code means."

Isabel coughed, rubbed her face, and opened her eyes. She smiled at Sage, both of them understanding the significance of the morning—their first together in Mexico.

"*Buenos dias*, Izzy-dactyl."

Isabel stretched. "*Buen dia*, Sage-asaurus."

"Happy birthday! I mean ... *¡feliz cumpleaños!*"

"*¡Gracias, amiga!*"

Sage inhaled deeply. "Something smells good!"

Isabel nodded. "*¡Chorizo!* I hope it's *con huevos* ... with eggs!"

"*¿Chorizo?*" Sage asked. "What's that?"

"It's Mexican sausage with chili peppers inside."

Sage's ears perked up with the mention of "chili peppers." "Sounds delicious!"

"It is," Isabel said as someone's stomach growled deeply. Isabel giggled. "Was that you or me?"

The bedroom door creaked as Mr. Carrington poked his head inside. "Anybody awake in here?"

Sage presented a huge smile to her dad and responded, "We are, Daddy."

Mr. Carrington entered the room, strode to the window, and gazed outside. "What a beautiful morning! Look at that sky. You kids are going to have a great time exploring the city today with Beatriz. The Zocalo, National Palace, and the Angel of Independence. And tonight, Isabel's birthday party." Sage smiled at Isabel, then sensed a streak of sadness in her dad. "Meanwhile, we're stuck in meetings all day. Oh well …" He turned to the girls. "Who's hungry?"

"What's for breakfast, Mr. C?"

"Chorizo, Isabel." He turned to Sage and winked. "One serving is extra spicy."

Sage flashed a brilliant smile. "Anything else on the menu?"

"Fresh tortillas, orange juice, rice, beans, and eggs."

"*¡Chorizo con huevos!*" Isabel said. "My favorite." She grabbed Sage's arm. "*Vamos*, Sage-asaurus."

"Okay, Izzy-dactyl." Sage caught her dad grinning at their prehistoric nicknames. He always seemed to be amused by the dino-talk.

Sage and Isabel scampered out of the room, and Mr. Carrington closed the door behind them. As Sage approached the kitchen, sounds of a sizzling skillet grew louder, and the spicy aroma of Mexican sausage filled her head. *Breakfast first,* she thought. *Then we'll explore Mexico City with Beatriz … and solve Frida's mystery.*

Sage and Isabel entered the dining room.

"There she is!"

"Happy birthday, Isabel!"

"Congratulations, sweetie!"

"*¡Feliz cumpleaños!*"

"Thanks everybody!" Isabel hugged and kissed her parents, before sitting next to Sage at the table.

"So, what is the answer to your riddle?" Manuel asked Isabel's mom.

"Oh ... yes," Mrs. Flores said. "And so that means *you're a peein'!*"

Sage looked at Isabel. "Izzy!"

Isabel snickered. "I didn't tell her. Promise!"

"*I* told her," Mrs. Carrington admitted with a smile and a shake of her head. "You kids and your jokes."

"Well, it's not *our joke*, Mommy." Sage pointed toward the bedroom. "It's from our cryptography book. Remember?"

"Cryptography?" Beatriz tilted her head. "What is this?"

"Well," Isabel began. "It's the science of codes."

"And ciphers," Sage added. "We're learning how to decrypt secret messages."

"Like spies!" Isabel said.

"Yeah, math spies!"

"Cryptograms. Ciphers," Beatriz repeated. "*¡Muy interestante!* I wonder, do you find any codes here in Mexico? We have a very country old."

Sage chuckled. "A *very old* country."

"Ahh!" Beatriz smiled. "A very old country. I am confused sometimes with the order of words! Thanks, *amiga*."

Sage loved the way Beatriz smiled. It wasn't just a facial expression, but more of an energy that seemed to radiate from her whole body. "*De nada.*"

"Well," Benji announced, while stuffing his mouth with rice, "there's the cryptogram we found in the Frida Kahlo painting."

"Benji!" Isabel said.

Bowls of food jumped on the table with a thud. "Owww!" Benji said, looking at Sage. "You kicked me!"

Sage couldn't believe Benji had spilled the beans about their secret. "Shhh!"

"What's that?" Mr. Carrington asked. "Frida Kahlo painting?"

"Yesterday?" Beatriz asked. "You locate something in *el museo*?"

Sage chuckled uncomfortably. "Well ... we just ... you know. We really enjoyed the museum. That's all Benji was trying to say." She shot him a piercing gaze then growled through clenched teeth, "Right ... Benji?"

"No, I was saying we found a crypto—" Another thud. More jumping food. "Owww!"

"Nefertari Sage Carrington!" her mom said.

Benji finally got the message. "Nevermind."

"*Nefertari?*" Beatriz pointed to Sage. "That is you?"

"Yep, it's my *real* first name. Sage is actually my middle name."

"Nefertari," Beatriz repeated with a glorious smile. "Like the queen of Egypt."

"You know who she was?"

"*Bueno,*" Beatriz chuckled. "I am a lover of history. I study all great people of the world."

Sage sent her a brilliant smile.

"I wonder ..." Manuel motioned to the adults. "You are all *scientistas?*"

"Yes, Manuel," Mr. Carrington said. "I'm a geologist. My wife's a chemist." He pointed to Isabel's parents. "Roberto studies astronomy. Carmen is an epidemiologist." He motioned to Benji. "Benji's parents—Alexandra and Rachel—study paleo-archeology and marine biology. We'll see them tomorrow at the Olmec ruins in San Lorenzo." He returned his attention to the table. "And Drusilla is a physicist."

"Yours is a very impressive team." Manuel reached for a covered dish and removed the lid to reveal a pile of dark chocolate candy. "For our guests, young and old, a special breakfast treat. Chocolate with *almendra.*"

"Almonds," Isabel said.

"*¡Delicioso!*" Sage added.

Benji licked his lips. "Candy!"

"Please, have some." Manuel smiled. "Do you know that chocolate was invented in Mexico?"

Benji reached for a piece of candy. "It was?"

Manuel nodded. "It is true. Many thousands of years ago."

Sage grabbed a piece of chocolate, but her mom leaned in. "I don't think so, young lady."

"Why not, Mommy?"

"Did you hear what Manuel said? It has *almonds* in it."

"Oh," Sage's energy deflated, "I forgot."

Beatriz grabbed a piece of candy. "You have allergy, Sage? With almonds?"

Sage shook her head. "It's not that. It's ..." she flashed a toothy smile, showing her metalwork to the table. "My braces. I can't eat any almonds ... or peanuts or potato chips ... chewing gum ... popcorn ... or—"

"That's enough, Sage," her mom said. "Just *be thankful* you have braces."

Sage heard Benji chomp on a piece of the candy. She couldn't quite tell if he was intentionally making all that noise just to rub it in.

Manuel turned to Isabel's dad. "And why are you here now in Mexico?"

Mr. Flores wiped his face and sipped his juice.

"Our colleagues across the region recently uncovered some impressive artifacts, and they're going to deliver presentations of their findings. We'll visit each site, attend the meetings, and take our notes back to the main offices in DC. This is important because we want the Smithsonian to understand how our research dollars are being spent here in Mexico." He motioned to the adults at the table. "We're one of the few interdisciplinary teams at the institution equipped to handle such complex work."

Benji froze mid-chew. "What's *interdisciplinary*?"

Mrs. Carrington leaned in. "That means our team has expertise in many different subjects ... different *disciplines*, dear."

Benji resumed chewing. "Gotcha, Mrs. C."

Manuel turned to the kids. "And today you all see the city with *mi* Beatriz."

Sage clapped her hands. "Yay!"

"We get wall-to-wall meetings," Mrs. Flores said to the adults. "And they get a walking tour of Mexico City."

Mrs. Carrington nodded. "Seems so unfair, Carmen."

Isabel leaned into Sage and said, "Seems fair to me."

"Yeah," Sage added. "Besides, that's what you all get for being brilliant scientists!"

Beatriz winked as the adults laughed. "*El Zócalo es muy bonito.* I show you *el Palacio Nacional* and *El Ángel de la Independencia.*"

"She wants to say our National Palace and the Angel of Independence." Manuel sipped a glass of water. "I try to remind *mi hjia* to speak in English, but she often forgets. Beatriz is daughter of mine ... and child of Mexico."

The table erupted with laughter as Manuel raised his glass. "To our friends and visitors, may you remain safe here in Mexico. And always travel with peace. *¡Salud!*"

"*¡Salud!*"

"*¡Salud, todo!*"

Glasses clinked.

Sage savored the moment as her thoughts returned to last night's discovery. *A real-life cryptogram from Frida Kahlo. I still can't believe it. But, we only have three more days to solve her mystery! Frida's next clue is somewhere in the Zocalo, and today we're going to find it.*

9

A Tour of El Zócalo

The late-morning sun shined above the Zocalo, a magnificent central square in the heart of Mexico City. Fluffy white clouds paraded overhead, and a steady breeze battled the summer heat. Cars jammed the streets, and pedestrians crowded the walkways as dancers, musicians, and other artists performed for camera-toting tourists who clapped and cheered to each remarkable twist, turn, and soaring melody.

"*Bienvendos al Zócalo,*" Beatriz said. "A most famous location in *Distrito Federal*, where many come to enjoy the city."

Benji raised his hand. "What's *Distrito Federal*?"

"Federal District," Beatriz answered. "I believe you have similar *en los Estados Unidos*. Washington, the District of Columbia, right? It is a federal district, not a state or a city."

"That's where we're from!" Isabel said.

"Yeah," Sage added. "We all live there!"

"*Genial!*" Beatriz smiled. "You live in the federal district *there*." She opened her arms wide to present the city square to the kids. "And I live in the federal district *here*. Do you know this city is built on an ancient lake?"

"Really!?"

"No!"

"Lake Texcoco," Beatriz said. "In the sixteenth century, the Spanish conquered this land and constructed a capital on top of what was once a great Aztec city called *Tenochtitlán*. In fact, it is due to the geology of this land that Mexico City is sinking today."

Sage hopped around, searching for signs of the earth dipping beneath her feet.

"Have no fear, Sage! The city sinks at a rate of fifteen to twenty centimeters per *year*."

Isabel drew several large numbers in the air while calculating. "That's about six to eight inches."

"*Eso.*"

Benji pointed to a reinforced stone building that occupied several city blocks. A collection of poles strewn across its rooftop anchored huge Mexican flags, which danced in the midday breeze. "What's that?"

"Our *Palacio Nacional*," Beatriz responded. "The National Palace." She thought for a moment. "It is similar, I believe, to your House White."

"House White?" Benji said.

"*Sí,*" Beatriz responded. "*Casa Blanca.* I believe it is where your president lives with his *familia.*"

"Oh!" Benji got it. "The White House!"

"*Eso.*" Beatriz snapped her fingers. "I must be careful with my order of words." She poked Benji's arm. "The *White House.* Thank you."

Sage noticed Benji blushing from Beatriz's touch.

"You're welcome." He shrugged, and then dragged his shoe across the concrete. "Anytime."

Suddenly the sound of a jingling bell was followed by a food cart racing past the group.

"Careful!" Beatriz instructed the kids as Isabel hopped out of the way. "People in the Zocalo move quite fast at times. Please look after your back."

"Beatriz," Sage smiled. "It's 'watch your back.'"

"Thank you, *querida.* Please *watch* your *back.*"

A thunderous boom echoed overhead. Sage looked up and saw a massive Mexican flag waving in the afternoon breeze. Especially strong gusts sent the fabric cracking like a whip. "That flag is huge!"

"It is one of the largest in all the world," Beatriz said. "The weight of this flag is seventy-five kilograms." She looked to Sage. "Do you know what this equals in *libras?*"

"*Libras?*" Benji asked.

Beatriz seemed confused. "You use *libras* in the

79

United States, no?" She touched her chin. "I think you write it as *l-b-s.*"

"L-b-s?" Benji repeated.

Sage hopped into the air. "Pounds!"

"*¡Eso!*" Beatriz clapped her hands. "Pounds, yes. American pounds."

"You call them *libras?*" Benji asked.

"*Claro.*"

"So that's where l-b-s comes from ... cool!"

"I forgot about that!" Isabel added. "I always say *kilograms* with my grandma."

"The many facts one learns in Mexico!" Beatriz said with a proud tone. "Okay, *mis niños*, tell me. Do you know how many *libras* ..." She paused, then rephrased with the more familiar word. "How many *pounds* this equals ... seventy-five kilograms?"

Sage looked to Isabel as both girls activated their mental calculators. "Let's see, one kilogram is equal to—"

"Two-point-two pounds." Isabel drew imaginary numbers in the air. "So, seventy-five kilograms equals—"

"Seventy-five times two," Sage said. "Which is 150—"

"Plus seventy-five times 0.2—"

"That's another fifteen—"

"So 150 plus fifteen is..."

Both girls answered together. "It's 165 pounds!"

They looked at each other, and then tossed in the same disclaimer. "*¡Más o menos!*"

"*¡Muy bien!*" Beatriz high-fived both girls. "I want you to look at the details of our national flag. Do you see the colors?"

Sage raised a hand to shield her eyes from the blinding sun and examined the three vertical blocks of color that composed the Mexican flag.

"The first stripe," Beatriz said, "is green. This is a symbol of our hope for a new country after we defeated Spain in the revolution of 1810. The second stripe is white for our purity of mind and spirit as we moved forward as an independent nation. Finally, the red stripe symbolizes the blood of Mexican heroes—men and women—who fought and died for our country. We remember their spirits always."

"And what's that inside the white stripe?" Sage said. "It looks like a bird."

"You are correct, Sage. This is the Mexican coat of arms, which shows a golden eagle, perched atop a pear cactus, eating a snake. This symbol was important to the Aztecs of *Tenochtitlán* with rich social, political, and religious significance."

Sage stared skyward as she walked into the flagpole's shadow. She heard Isabel clicking photos nearby, but couldn't unglue her eyes from the flag. Brilliant sunlight sparkled through the textured fabric, and the bright sky seemed to make the flag look darker. She couldn't discriminate the flag's colors; it was now like a shadowy silhouette. In the blinding light, she stood mesmerized by the wavering shapes of the huge fabric as it danced to the rhythm of Mexico's summer winds.

Then a magnificent pillar behind the flagpole drew her attention. Perched atop the pillar, a golden, winged woman stood on one foot, while extending her arm toward the national palace. "Who is she?"

Beatriz followed Sage's gaze. "Ah, yes. Is beautiful, no? She is the Angel of Independence. A symbol of our victory during the revolution."

"Is *she* the woman you were named after ... Beatriz Gonzales Ortega?"

"Perhaps. But one must remember ... we had *many* angels during the war. Beatriz Ortega was but one. Come, let's go to the National Palace." The group started walking toward the building. "And are you aware that many states in America were once part of Mexico?"

"Which ones?" Benji said.

"California," Beatriz said. "New Mexico, Arizona, Nevada, Utah—"

"They were all *Mexican* states?"

"*Sí*, Benjamin. All lost after Mexico surrendered to America in the War of 1846."

"We had a war?"

"The Army of the United States marched into Mexico City—to this very site. The American soldiers lowered the Mexican flag and, to celebrate victory, raised the American Stars and Stripes high above *el Zócalo*."

"That's unbelievable!"

"In 1848, Mexico agreed to the Treaty of Guadeloupe Hidalgo, which transferred those five complete states–the ones I described. Additionally, America received more land to increase the size of Kansas, Oklahoma, Wyoming, and Colorado. Oh, I and forget ... Texas was *also* a state of Mexico. Well, until the year 1836, when it revolted and created an independent republic."

"No way! Texas was a part of Mexico, too?"

"It is true. And after finding its independence, another ten years passed before the Republic of Texas joined the United States as its twenty-eighth state."

"I never knew any of that," Sage said.

Isabel shook her head. "Me neither."

"These events are part of the historical record," Beatriz said. "I encourage you to learn more. It is important to study history, *amigos*. For it is our memory of the past that guides us, like a compass, into the future."

The group continued darting between vendors, taxis, and scurrying pedestrians as they arrived at the entrance to the National Palace. Several uniformed military guards flanked a stone archway. They strolled past the guards and arrived at an interior courtyard. An intricate stone fountain rested beside two magnificent marble staircases leading to upper levels of the palace.

"Should we go left or right?" Beatriz asked.

"I'm going right." Benji began walking.

"Well, I'm going left. You righties get everything," Sage said, with pride in her left-handedness. "So I choose to go left whenever possible!"

"*Claro, amiga,*" Isabel said. "Then I'm going left too."

"Oh, well, I guess I can go left too," Benji agreed.

"You go to left," Beatriz said. "And to make a point, I go to right. Let us meet up the stairs. Okay?"

The kids nodded, and Sage watched Beatriz walk to the far side of the atrium and start upstairs.

"Sage! Come on!" Benji shouted.

As she trotted to the staircase, Sage noticed that the steps were incredibly wide. She extended both arms to measure the width, but her span didn't even account for half of the staircase. The railing was nearly as tall as she was, and it felt cold against her palm. She arrived at a landing halfway between the first and second floors and found Isabel and Benji frozen in place, mouths dangling open.

"What are you guys looking at..."

Oh my goodness. She gazed at a massive mural

full of people, places, and events. It reminded her of a wall-sized comic book. *This is ... I've never ... I can't believe ... the size ... it's the whole wall!*

"Pssst! Pssst!" Beatriz, who had met them at the landing, motioned to the mural and whispered, "Diego Rivera."

"Is Frida in this one?" Isabel scream-whispered to Beatriz. "Did Diego paint her?"

"She is here." Beatriz pointed to the top of the wall. "In *el medio* up there. Do you see?"

Sage squinted her eyes. "It's too far away. I can't see way up there."

"Me neither." Isabel snapped her fingers. "But I have my telephoto!" She dipped a hand into her backpack and replaced the lens on her camera.

"See anything, Izzy?"

"I ... I do!" She snapped several pictures. "It's Frida! She's here!" She lowered her camera, adjusted several dials, and returned it to her face. *Click. Click.* "This faster shutter speed should help to reduce any blur."

"What about the cipher? Do you see any more symbols?" The anticipation was killing Sage.

Isabel gasped. "I ... I do!"

"What *are* they?"

"They look similar to the characters from the painting ... from *The Two Fridas*."

"Can I see?"

Isabel lowered the camera and handed it to Sage. "Careful, that's my favorite lens!"

Sage cradled the camera, raised it to her face, and gazed through the viewfinder. Diego's vivid mural occupied the full frame. His measured brush strokes and luscious colors leapt to life. Sage's pulse raced as she located the ciphertext painted below Frida's feet. "I can't stop shaking, Izzy. I can't read a thing."

"You have to calm down, Sage-asaurus. Deep breaths."

Sage followed Isabel's direction but couldn't calm her nerves. The image in the camera's viewfinder jumped with each beat of her pounding heart. "I ... can't ... It's just too blurry right now."

"I know what you mean. That's one of the hardest things to do in photography—to hold still when working with a long telephoto lens. Even I have trouble, sometimes. Plus, that cipher is super small."

Sage handed the camera back to Isabel.

"But don't worry. I have pictures now. And we'll develop them later tonight at my aunt's house, in Victor's homemade photo room. We can enlarge the prints and see *exactly* what Frida's trying to tell us."

It was during times like these that Sage wished Isabel would just get a digital camera already. *If she used digital, then we could see the pictures right now! Besides, what's so great about photographing on film anyway?*

Ding. Dong.

Ding. Dong.

Sage froze to the sound of the tolling bell. "What's that?"

Ding. Dong.

"*El Cathedral Nacional*," Beatriz responded with a smile. "It is the bell of the National Cathedral. She glanced at her watch. "We must leave for a visit to the great pyramids of Mexico. The van arrives *en un momento* to carry us there." She extended both hands to Sage and Benji. Isabel snapped a final series of pictures, and the group began back down the stone staircase. "I will show you the great ancient city of Teotihuacan. And I promise, you will never forget."

10

Pyramids at Teotihuacan

The afternoon sun had burned away any lingering clouds, and a clear sky rested above the ancient site. Sage basked in the warm air and also noticed a mild tingling sensation in her chest; it wasn't painful or scary. On the contrary, it was a pleasant, calm feeling. Something was different about this place. The energy. The atmosphere. She had difficulty pinpointing exactly what *it* was; nonetheless, *it* was present at Teotihuacan.

As she walked through the valley of the Teotihuacan ruins, her thoughts remained on Diego's mural from the National Palace. *I wonder what Frida's second cipher says. Will it be based on the same polynumeric code as before? We have to wait until we arrive in Veracruz tonight to develop Izzy's pictures and to decipher the message. But I don't want to wait!*

She raised a palm to shade her eyes while gazing into the brilliant sky. A pair of condors glided above, their enormous wings spanning to infinity. More tingles filled her body as she observed how effortlessly the majestic birds soared. She closed her eyes and inhaled deeply. With each breath, she imagined air entering her nostrils and traveling into her lungs.

"Sage-asaurus!" Isabel scampered over. "Did you see it yet? It's amazing! Super amazing! *More* than super amazing!" She held up her camera. "These photos are epic!"

Sage snapped out of her daydream and found Isabel approaching fast. Before she could respond, Isabel had snatched her hand and pulled her farther along the valley floor.

"You're not gonna believe this!" They turned a corner and froze.

An immense stone pyramid ascended to the heavens. "Izzy, it's … it's …" Sage couldn't find the words to fully convey her thoughts and feelings. She had wanted to say *awesome, incredible, amazing,* but she couldn't find a clear thought. The pyramid was awe-inspiring, and she couldn't grasp any of the words streaming through her overflowing brain. She blurted out the first mish-mash of sounds that entered her mind. "It's … *fantabuloso!*"

Isabel laughed at Sage's new vocabulary. *"Muy fantabuloso!"*

"The Pyramid of the Sun," Beatriz said from behind. "The base of the pyramid is seventy square meters, approximately the same size as the Great Pyramid on the Giza Plateau in Egypt. However, this pyramid is seventy-one meters tall, about half the height of the Great Pyramid."

"Is it as old as the Egyptian pyramids?"

"No, Sage. The Giza pyramids in Egypt were constructed nearly five thousand years ago. This pyramid was constructed two thousand years ago, *más o menos.*"

"Amazing!"

"Even more amazing ... this pyramid remained the tallest building in the Americas for more than 1,800 years until the Trinity Church was constructed in New York City."

"Beatriz, have you ever been to New York?"

"Or Egypt?" Sage added.

"No ... and no. But it is my dream. And you?"

"Not yet."

"Nope."

"Well, if one day you go, then you must return to Mexico and share fantastic stories with me."

"Okay!"

"Deal!"

Beatriz pointed down a road that led to another

pyramid on the far side of the complex. "That is the Pyramid of the Moon. And many refer to this as 'the avenue of the dead', but I do not like the name. Instead, I call it *la calle de Dios.*"

"The road of God," Isabel said.

Beatriz smiled. "This *calle* is aligned perfectly to magnetic north of the Earth's axis. To this point, the design is no accident. This city is a grid, a quadrangle."

Sage gasped. "Like Washington, DC!"

"The temples and two hundred smaller pyramids are all ordered to the sun, moon, and other heavenly bodies. Before a single stone was moved, the engineers organized each detail for the benefit of future residents to live, learn, and pray in comfort. Teotihuacan is constructed after thousands of years of studying geometry, astronomy, and mathematics."

"Who built all this?"

"We are not certain. But I believe the architects were touched by God. They possessed a unique energy, knowledge, and observation of the natural world, which dates back to the Olmec people almost four thousand years ago."

"Was it a popular place to live?

"We estimate that in the year 450 more than 150,000 people occupied more than 2,000 residential buildings—multifamily housing—across an area of twenty square kilometers."

"A metropolis!"

"*Sí*, Sage. Teotihuacan was a shining light to the world. Many visitors would come from thousands of kilometers in all directions to live here. At this time in history, the city is more populous than Athens in Greece and larger than Rome in Italy."

"So why did they build these pyramids?" Sage asked.

"Yeah," Isabel said. "What's their purpose?"

"Well, we do not know exactly why. It is believed perhaps the pyramids were astronomical laboratories to view the heavens, or temples or tombs. Maybe even power plants. Perhaps a combination of all four. We simply do not know for certain."

"*Power plants?*"

"You will learn, Sage. The energy here is special, unlike other locations in the world."

"What happened to the people who lived here?"

"This is also a mystery. We know the residents disappeared in the ninth century. But we do not know the cause. Perhaps a hurricane, earthquake, disease, or other peculiar disaster."

Sage thought for a moment. "Sort of like how the Maya disappeared?"

"Exactly," Beatriz chuckled. "It seems my country is full of mysteries."

"We love mysteries!"

"After its fall, the Aztecs discovered an empty

city, and they named it Teotihuacan. To the present day, it remains the most popular archaeological site for visitors."

Isabel grabbed Sage's hand and started sprinting toward the structure. "Let's climb the Pyramid of the Sun!" Her camera swished back and forth with each step. "I *have* to get some shots from the top!"

"Hi, Mommy! Hey, Dad!" Sage shouted, as she passed her parents. She heard the adults mutter something about being careful as Isabel continued pulling. The girls reached the base of the pyramid and hopped up its first steps. She released Isabel's hand and placed a palm on the stone structure. The rock fired a radiant bolt of pleasure up her arm. Her entire body felt warmer. "Izzy, do you feel that?"

Isabel put a hand beside Sage's and flinched. "Well, I know one thing."

"What's that?" Sage asked, hearing Beatriz's voice repeat in her head, *a power plant.*

"There are some things I can photograph and other things I can't."

"This feeling. The energy here—"

"I can't take a picture of it."

"You just have to *be* here."

Isabel nodded. "And feel it for yourself."

"Let's go to the top!" Sage said. "Come on!" She trailed Isabel as the girls climbed past the slower-moving patrons.

"We have to get some pictures up there!"

As they ascended, Sage felt the pyramid's energy intensifying. *Can rocks create electricity?* she wondered. *I don't remember learning that in school. Or maybe certain places in the world have special electrical powers?* Her scientific mind sought an explanation. With each step higher, fantastic jolts of pleasure traveled up her legs.

"We're getting close to the top, Izzy!"

She imagined the pyramid's energy spreading throughout her body. *Maybe it's a closed system, like a copper wire connecting the positive and negative terminals of a battery to a shining light bulb. Are my legs like the copper wire?* she wondered. *So then, am I the light bulb? And if that's true, then does that mean the pyramid is a battery?* She shook her head. *Can't be ... can it?*

"We're here!" she wiped sweat from her forehead as they hopped the final steps.

Click. Click. Click. Isabel wasted no time photographing panoramas from their rarified perspective.

At the higher altitude, streams of wind whipped against Sage's face. She squinted to protect her eyes and searched for the rest of the group on the ground level. A familiar band of spectators caught her attention. "There they are!" she said, standing on her toes and waving both arms. "Hello, down there!" In the howling wind, she realized they probably couldn't hear anything from so far away. "Izzy, get a picture of our parents!"

Isabel spun, focused her camera, and fired off several shots of the valley. "How high are we?" she asked.

"Beatriz said the pyramid is seventy-one meters high. Times 3.3 ... that's—"

Both girls responded at the same time. "That's about 230 feet ... more or less!"

They hugged atop the pyramid as a familiar voice traveled up the stone structure. "Sage! Isabel!" Benji huffed. "Come on! Our parents said it's time to go. The van to Veracruz is coming."

Sage peeked over the side of the plateau and saw him trudging up the steps, panting.

"We're going to see my moms at the Olmec site on the coast," he said. "And then ... Isabel's party tonight."

"Izzy, your birthday!" Sage reminded herself.

"*Sí, mi amiga,*" Isabel said. "*Esta noche.*"

"Happy birthday again, Izzy-dactyl," Sage said.

"*Gracias*, Sage-asaurus."

Hey, even the greatest detectives take a night off to celebrate a best friend's birthday, Sage thought. "*Vamos*, Izzy. Time to visit the Olmec site!"

11

Lessons from the Olmecs

A beige cloud of dust blanketed the barren landscape as a toiling crew quarried the site. Clanking sounds from their shovels, pickaxes, and rakes rippled through the afternoon air. Some workers wore handkerchiefs over the faces, while others sported goggles; a few wore no protection at all.

Sage spotted a group sitting on the ground with small brushes, gently sweeping dirt from excavated artifacts while others chiseled away with small hammer-like instruments.

"Well, howdy doody!" a female shouted from within the dust bowl.

Mrs. Carrington waved a hand in front of her face. "Alex!"

Alexandra Woodson emerged from the cloud, goggles dangling around her neck. The dirt stained her cheeks, chin, and forehead, but her eye sockets remained clean as googles had protected them.

"Mommy!" Benji dashed to Alex. It was the fastest sprint Sage had ever witnessed from her friend.

Alex bent down and received him with a loving hug. Then she examined him. "Two eyes. Two ears. A nose. Oh, I missed you, sweetie!" Alex froze. "Wait a second ... are you *really* my son?" She passed a hand from her shoulder to Benji's. "You look taller and slightly older. I know ... you're a fake. Well, I'll just have to tickle this imposter until my beloved son returns."

Benji shook his head. "It's me, Mommy!" The tickling sent him into a fit of laughter. "I'm Benjamin!"

Alex paused. "You are?"

"Yeah! Promise!"

She thought for a moment, and then resumed the tickling. "Nice try! But that's *exactly* what an imposter would say!"

"Really, it's me!"

She stopped again. "Well, okay. I guess it's you then." She looked at the group. "Whew ... that was a close call!"

"Mommy, you should have been there!" Benji spoke a hundred miles an hour; his memories collided with one another in a high-speed mental pileup. "The sunset from the airplane. Zocalo. Oh, and Frida's house ... all that traffic! Spicy sausage with eggs. The Pyramid of the Sun. And the tamales on the highway. Plus we saw this ginormous wall painting by Diego in the National Palace." He took a much-needed breath of air.

"Wow." Alex kissed Benji's hand. "Sounds like you've had some great adventures, my little prince." She stroked his hair. "I missed you so much, angel." She hugged and kissed him again, then looked at Sage.

"Hi, Ms. Alex!"

"Hello, Sage dear." Alex leaned in. "And what are you giggling at?"

Ms. Alex is sooo funny! Sage thought.

"Wait a sec," Alex said. "I know. It's ... the giggle monster. He's got you? Don't worry—" She turned her head and shouted into the distance. "We have a giggle monster sighting!"

Sage exploded with laughter.

"This giggle monster's tough," Alex began. "Only, one way to beat him. You know what it is?"

Sage nearly burst with anticipation.

"The answer is ... blurbling!" Alex pressed her lips against Sage's cheek and blew forcefully, sending a huge fart sound into the air. "Get out of her, giggle monster!" Another blow. "I command you to leave this child's body. Out, monster! Out, out, out!"

Sage was being blurbled, and she nearly fainted with laughter. Isabel snapped dozens of photos as the piercing fart sounds and group's laughter rose above the monotonous chiseling hammers in the distance.

As she settled down and released Sage, Alex became more serious, like a judge preparing to deliver the sentence in a courtroom. She stood up and straightened her hair and clothes. "I've exorcised the giggle monster," she announced in the most somber tone. "Worry no more, child." She brushed her hands together. "This site ... is clean."

Sage tossed both arms around Alex in the biggest hug imaginable.

"So, Mommy," Benji said. "How's the dig going?"

Alex squatted to the ground. "Hop up," she said, and Benji jumped on her back as the group began to walk. "We've excavated about 60 percent of the site and located all kinds of radical jewelry, tools, and groovy remains." She turned to Mr. Carrington. "In fact yesterday, Bruce, we recovered a fantastic set of medical instruments. Real Olmec tech. I'm talking clamps, tweezers, and scalpels—the same stuff used all over the world today."

The group arrived at a tent, where Alex squatted and instructed Benji to hop off her back. "Over here," she said, "Last week's findings." She led the team to a smooth white table with several items organized across its surface.

Sage squeezed between Mr. and Mrs. Flores for a front-row view. The surgical knives looked familiar.

They were just like the ones she'd seen in hospitals: long, slender handles with curved blades on their tips. Ditto for the tweezers. *I have a set of those in my room at home*, she thought.

"Those metal blades look funny," Benjamin said.

"These aren't metal, sweetie." His mom picked up a scalpel. "The cutting surface is obsidian—a shard of very sharp glass."

"What's the dating?" Mrs. Carrington asked.

"Preliminary carbon from the wooden handle indicates 1200 BCE," Alex responded. "But we're waiting on the official results from DC."

Benji's eyes lit up, "Mommy, this stuff is old. It's prehistoric!"

"You're looking at artifacts from the first documented civilization in the Americas. Before the Maya, Aztecs, Zapotecs, or Incas. The mighty Olmecs lived in the early dawn of American history. And, dear, these items—this civilization—are not 'prehistoric.' To be accurate, they are pre-Spanish."

"How long ago did the Olmecs live?" Sage asked.

"We believe they came onto the scene around 1500 BCE," Alex responded. "They flourished in this southern region of San Lorenzo and also thrived in two other sites—Tres Zapotes and La Venta—until about 400 BCE."

Mr. Carrington pointed to the table full of artifacts. "It's amazing how medical technology has advanced ... yet remained largely the same."

Mrs. Flores nodded. "Well, if it ain't broke—"

"Then don't even *think* about fixing it!" a female voice said from the tent's entrance.

Sage spun around and saw Rachel Woodson. Although it wasn't the most traditional household in the world, Benji and his two adoptive moms formed one of the most loving families Sage had ever seen.

"Wait ... is that how you say it?" Rachel approached the group. "I get my clichés mixed up sometimes. The kettle calls the black cat lucky ... two in the hand is worth more because three's a crowd."

"Mommy!" Benji shouted, as he raced from Alexandra to Rachel.

"My baby," Rachel said, smothering Benji with a hug. "Let me get a good look at you. Two eyes. A nose." She turned his head side to side. "Both ears." She looked at Mrs. Carrington. "Lorraine, you done real good, getting my son here safely."

Mrs. Carrington nodded. "My pleasure. Well ..." She motioned to the group. "*Our* pleasure."

"Of course," Rachel responded. "Thank you *all*."

"So, how's the dig going, Rach?"

"One benefit of being a paleontologist *and* archeologist is that I have the honor of working with the most incredible people on Earth. Team's been out there eight hours a day for the past two months, making some amazing discoveries. Come on. I'll show you."

Alex grabbed Rachel's hand as they led the group around the site.

"We're learning more about this great civilization every day," Rachel said.

"But, Mommy," Benji said. "I thought you studied the oceans."

"Yes, dear," Rachel said. "Marine biology ... with an archeological focus. We have reason to believe that these lands might have been covered by the ocean thousands of years ago."

"No way!"

"We're constantly learning new information about our world, honey. And about its civilizations."

"What are you learning about *this* civilization ... the Olmecs?"

"Well, until recently, the consensus in the scientific community was that the Olmecs used stone-based tools. You know, primitive stuff that would crack and break after a few uses. Watch your step—"

"But we now believe that's false," Alex said. "Olmec civilization was advanced. Highly technical.

We know because of what they built ... and what they discovered."

"Like what?" Isabel asked.

The group arrived at a massive stone statue in the shape of a head. As Sage stood beside the sculpture she realized it was several feet taller than she was.

Alex pointed to the statue. "Like these colossal stone heads. So far, about twenty of these heads have been discovered. Each is carved from solid basalt, with heights ranging from five to eleven feet, and weights anywhere from six to fifty *tons*."

"No way!" Sage said.

"Yep, this statue you're looking at is eight feet tall and weighs twenty tons. Anyone know how many pounds that is?"

Sage activated her mental calculator. "Well, there are 2,000 pounds in a ton ... times twenty tons, equals ..."

Isabel joined in and the girls responded together. "Forty thousand pounds!"

Alex cleared her ear with a finger. "Is there an echo out here?"

Sage and Isabel giggled and added, "More or less!"

"And check out these markings on the stone," Alex said. "We can see that they used advanced tools to quarry, transport, and carve each colossal head."

"So, how'd they do it," Sage asked. "How did the Olmecs build these giant statues?"

Alex shook her head. "To this day, hon, we don't know." She pointed to the distance. "Just like we're also searching for answers about the great pyramid builders in ancient Egypt. We're still trying to figure out how that incredible civilization quarried *millions* of stones, that each weighed two tons on average, then constructed pyramids so exact that to this day, you can't slip a sheet of paper between the stones."

Rachel wrapped her arms around Benji. "The world is full of wonder and mystery."

"Ms. Alex, is this what the Olmecs looked like?"

"Well, Sage, our best evidence is that these colossal heads were created in the images of the upper tier of their thinkers, political leaders, and warriors. We can only speculate—but yes, the consensus is that these monuments represented important figures in Olmec society."

"The facial features. And the head shape," Sage said. "They're very … distinct."

Ms. Alex nodded. "You are correct, my dear … and not the first to notice. In fact, anthropologist Jose Melgar made a point, during his first sighting of the colossal heads in the 1860s, to say that their features were of the 'Ethiopic type.' And did you know that the Olmecs were the first civilization

104

in the Western Hemisphere to develop a system of writing? Check this out." She pointed to several large symbols chiseled into the side of the head.

Sage examined the characters from every angle, but couldn't decipher their meanings. "What does it say?"

"This inscription is actually a long-count calendar ... another first for the Western Hemisphere. Even though we know the Egyptians had already developed an accurate calendar in Africa, the Olmec long-count calendar is the earliest of the Americas."

"But how do you know all of this stuff?" Benji asked. "I mean, who's to say that's a calendar and not ... a recipe for macaroni and cheese?"

Sage rolled her eyes. "Benji!"

"I'm serious! How do you *really* know what you *think* you know?"

Alex returned her attention to the inscriptions. "Well, honey, sometimes we don't know exactly what something means. Not at first, anyway. Language is constantly evolving, and the meaning of letters and symbols can change throughout time. That's why we spend years examining these artifacts. We're looking for patterns; searching for meaning."

"And in time," Rachel said, "the answers will appear. And they're usually in the smallest details."

"Often staring you right in the face," Alex added.

Rachel laughed. "Ain't that the truth!"

"You just have to keep trying, dear, and don't give up."

Benji returned his attention to the stone head. "So ... you're *sure* this isn't mac and cheese?"

The crowd erupted in laughter. "Yes, babe, we're sure." Alex rubbed Benji's stomach. "All this food talk can only mean one thing."

His stomach growled as Mrs. Carrington snapped a photo of the stone head. "Alex, Rach, you joining us for dinner tonight? We have a *birthday* to celebrate!"

A chorus of oooohhhhs emerged as Alex wrapped an arm around Isabel. "How could we resist the final hours of Princess Isabel's preteen life?" Alex lowered her head in sadness. "May your inner twelve year old rest in peace." She then raised a fist and nodded in excitement. "And the new thirteen year old ... rock on! Because it's party time! Par-tay!" She grabbed Isabel's hand and twirled the birthday girl. "Party, party, party!"

Rachel poked Sage's shoulder. "You're next, right? The big one-three. And with our new project, it looks like you'll be celebrating teenage-hood in Rio de Janeiro."

"Rio?" Mrs. Carrington said. "What do you mean?"

Alex and Rachel seemed confused. "You didn't see yesterday's announcement? It's hot off the press!"

"We've been running nonstop since yesterday morning," Mr. Flores said. "*What* announcement?"

"From the Smithsonian," Alex said. "Tony sent the news. Our next project—"

"A breakthrough on Luzia," Rachel said. "So next week we're going to Brazil!"

The group buzzed with excitement.

"Brazil!"

"Really?

"No way!"

"Rio!"

"Mommy," Benji said. "What's *Luzia?*"

"It's a twelve-thousand-year-old skeleton that was discovered in Brazil in the 1970s. Luzia is a very important piece of the human puzzle, because her remains are among the oldest ever found on the continent."

"The institution wants us to visit, confirm all research, and return with our findings."

Sage's spirit lit up. "*Brazil*, Izzy! Can you believe it?"

"Somebody pinch me, please," Isabel said. "Rio de Janeiro!?"

"But that's not all," Rachel said. "Our flights to Rio depart from JFK International Airport ... in New York City. So we plan to go directly from here to New York and stay there for a few days—"

"Yes," Alex said. "And then fly from New York to Rio in the middle of next week." She ran a hand across Benji's head. "What do you think, sweetie? A weekend in New York City?"

"Of course!"

"New York?" Drusilla said. "My hometown."

Alex nodded. "You're a Brooklyn girl, right?"

"Born and raised."

"Bruce, Lorraine … Roberto, Carmen … will you join us?"

In that moment, Sage knew two things for certain. One, they were absolutely going to solve Frida's mysterious messages. And two, she would do everything in her power in the next ten seconds to ensure that her parents answered with a 'yes.' "Mommy! Daddy! Please! Please, please, please!"

Isabel began working on her parents too. "Yeah, Mommy! Can we, Dad? Pleeease!"

"It'll be great," Rachel winked at Sage. "One happy research family."

Sage looked at her parents, who seemed to be in agreement with Rachel. They glanced at Sage and appeared to be fully convinced by her boisterous energy.

"The Big Apple, dear?" Mr. Carrington said.

Mrs. Carrington nodded. "Let's take a bite."

"We're in too," Mr. Flores said.

"Yes!"

"Yay!"

"Well, this calls for a celebration!" Mr. Carrington said.

"New York, Izzy!" Sage excitedly turned to her friend.

"It's official," Isabel said. "Rio ... New York ... I'm *totally* dreaming!"

Mr. Flores looked at his watch. "Speaking of celebrations, guys, we should get going if we want to make it to my sister's house for the big party."

Sage leaned against Isabel. "Birthday girl!"

"The van's probably waiting," Mr. Flores said, as the group started toward the site's entrance.

Sage began walking, then looked back at the colossal Olmec head, still amazed by the size and weight of the massive sculpture. She wondered how the Olmecs could have cut, lifted, and carried such a large stone. *The world is full of wonder and mystery*, she remembered Rachel saying. Then Alex: *We're looking for patterns ... the answers will appear ... in the smallest details ... staring you right in the face ... you just have to keep trying ... and don't give up.*

Sage smiled. *I know exactly what you mean, Ms. Alex. That's how I feel about Frida's cryptogram!* She turned her attention to Isabel. *We'll be patient, and we won't give up. Not a chance.* She shook her head and cleared her mind. *But now ... it's time to celebrate my best friend's birthday.*

12

Izzy's Party

The setting sun shimmered on the ocean's surface. Sage moseyed into the water and closed her eyes as the breeze danced across her cheeks and continued down the shoreline. A dull woo-ing sound soothed her ears, and the salty aroma wafted into her nostrils. With each gust, a sweet film accumulated on her lips. She opened her eyes and followed a fleet of wooden canoes drifting beyond the breaking waves. The men inside the boats twirled their arms overhead, like rodeo cowboys preparing to lasso a runaway bull.

"*Pescadores*," Isabel said from behind her. She joined Sage at the water's edge. "Fishermen."

Sage nodded. "But they're just using fishing line. Where are the poles?"

"You know how Mrs. Armstrong always tells us in homeroom that there's more than one way to skin a cat?"

"Yeah."

Isabel smiled. "Well, there's also more than one way to catch a fish."

"That's true, birthday girl. Hey, let me have a look at you." Sage pretended to give Isabel a physical exam. "Hair looks good, like a thirteen year old's. Yep, smile is teen-ish." She shoved her face into Isabel's. "Okay, now open your mouth wide and say 'ahhhhhh.'"

Isabel tapped Sage on the arm. "Very funny, Sage-saurus!"

Sage wrapped both of her arms around one of Isabel's. "So, how does it feel?"

Isabel shrugged. "Same as yesterday, when I was still twelve."

"Well ... *I'm* twelve, and *you're* thirteen." Sage laughed. "So that means you're a year older than I am now!"

"Not even, Sage-asaurus. Only by a few days."

"Okay, true. Less than a week to go for me."

"And it looks like we'll be celebrating your birthday on the beach in Rio de Janeiro!"

"Do you really think we'll go? I *still* can't believe it, Izzy."

"I know!" Isabel looked intensely at Sage. "Hey, now that I think about it, you *do* have the eyes of a twelve year old." She pinched Sage's ear. "Yep, ears too." Isabel shoved her face into Sage's. "Now open your mouth and say 'ahhhhhhh.'"

Sage loved when Isabel turned her jokes around. "No way! Stop, Izzy!"

"Thirteen," Isabel said in disbelief.

"Yep, teenagers now. And there's no turning back. Like a tattoo on the face, it's here to stay." She sensed a wave of sadness overcoming Isabel. "What is it, Izzy-dactyl?"

Isabel shook her head. "It's just ... we're not little girls anymore, you know? It's like Beatriz said ... we're *young women* now."

Sage related to Isabel's somber mood. "Yeah. And do you feel ... *funny*? Like someone's doing science experiments inside your body?"

"Exactly! It's like I'm a walking, talking chemistry set! I just feel—"

Whoosh!

An intense burst of heat rushed up Sage's back, and a massive fireball billowed into the sky. Two men stood nearby, and, in the smoke-filled haze, Sage forgot about her conversation with Isabel. Instead, she watched in amazement while the men skewered a series of chickens and a whole pig. The men attached the meat to a homemade roaster, which was built atop a colossal fire pit. The flames receded, replaced by plumes of smoke. A large food tent was set up beside them, and Sage's stomach rumbled at the sight of rice, beans, salad, fruit, and vegetables.

Behind the girls, a collection of chairs and tables surrounded an open space, which was fashioned into a dance floor. A mariachi band's valiant horns and pulsing strings sliced through the humid air as revelers spun, hopped, and danced beneath a banner that read: *!FELIZ CUMPLEAÑOS, ISABEL!* Sage watched the festivities and imagined that the whole community was present: kids, parents, grandparents, and even great-grandparents. It looked like every resident of Veracruz was attending Isabel's birthday celebration.

Another stomach rumble.

"Was that you or me?" Isabel grabbed Sage's hand.

"Definitely *me*."

Benji joined the girls. "This is a great party!"

"Hey, Benji-raptor!" Sage said. "You hungry?"

"Yes!" He spun to follow Sage and Isabel as—

"Watch out!"

A girl slammed into him. The two kids fell to the ground, and a Frisbee landed nearby.

Benji replaced his glasses and then shifted his attention to the careless, running girl. "Hey, what are you thinking, smashing into me like that? You should look where you're going!"

Sage watched the girl reach for the Frisbee before focusing her attention on Benji. "*Lo siento!*"

she said. "*Es que ...*" She froze.

Benji waved a hand in front of her face, just like Sage had done when he'd met Beatriz yesterday. In fact, Sage noticed the same goofy expression on this girl's face. "Hello?" he said. "Anybody home?" He tossed both hands into the air. "Great, she can't speak."

The girl's eyes batted, and she seemed to return to the moment. "*¡Hola!*" A huge smile covered her face, and her eyes softened. "*¿Cómo estas? Bienvenidos a Veracruz.*" She kissed him on the left cheek, smiled brilliantly, then kissed his other cheek. "*Mi nombre es Escarlet. Un placer conocerte.*" The girl appeared to search for words. "My name is Escarlet. It is a pleasure for know you."

"A pleasure *to* know you," Benji corrected.

Escarlet flashed a beaming smile. "*Muchas gracias.*" She remained fixated on him while fiddling with the Frisbee in her hands.

"*¡Prima!*" Isabel tossed both arms around Escarlet. "*¿Cómo estas?* How are you?" The girls kissed cheeks.

"Isabel! I am very fine," Escarlet responded. "How are you?"

"Great!" Isabel spun around. "Hey, Sage, this is my cousin, Escarlet."

"*Un placer.*" She kissed Escarlet's cheeks. "*Mi nombre es Sage.*"

"A pleasure, Sage." With her accent, it sounded like Escarlet was saying *Say-sh*.

Isabel pivoted to Benji. "*Y él es mi amigo, Benjamin.*"

"*Hola*, Benjamin," Escarlet said with a blush. She pronounced the *j* in his name like an *h*: *Ben-ha-min*.

"Nice to meet you," he responded. His stomach joined Sage's in a chorus of growls.

"*¿Ustedes tienen hambre?*" Escarlet asked. "You are ... with hunger?"

"*¡Sí!*"

"*¡Muy!*"

"Yes!"

"*Entonces, vamos a comer.*" Escarlet led them to the food tent and handed plates to Isabel and Sage. She then stood next to Benji and personally assisted with his plate preparation.

Sage couldn't help but chuckle at Benji's new admirer. "How old is Escarlet?" she asked Isabel.

"Let's see, she's three years younger than me. I'm thirteen, so Escarlet must be ten."

Sage chuckled. "That's *perfect*. Benji's eleven and Escarlet's ten. Oh, this is gonna be a fun night."

"*¿Quieres pollo, Ben-ha-min?*" Escarlet asked. "*Pollo* is ... chicken."

Benji looked a bit uncomfortable with all this new attention, but he seemed to take it all in stride. Sage figured that since he'd had a long day, he appreciated the kindness. "Yes—I mean, *sí. Por favor.*"

"Rice?"

"*Sí.*"

"*¿Ensalada?*"

"*Sí.*"

Escarlet continued the questions and answers as she piled food onto his plate. "*¿Y para tomar?*"

"*¿Tomar?* I don't understand." He looked to Isabel for a translation.

"She wants to know what you want to drink."

"Oh," Benji said while scanning the options. "I'll have juice." He pointed to the punch bowl. "*Por favor.*"

Escarlet filled his cup. "*Jugo de tamarindo ... ¿ésta bien?*"

He looked to Isabel again.

"Tamarind juice, Benji-raptor."

"Hmm, never had it before but ..." He shrugged. "Sure. I'll try it."

"It's yummy!" Isabel said. "And my aunt makes the best." She looked at Escarlet. "*El jugo de tamarindo de tu mama es lo mejor.*"

Escarlet's face lit up. "*Sí, prima. ¡Con certeza!*"

Sage piled rice and beans on her plate and placed several pieces of roasted chicken on top. She then reached for a large cup of the legendary tamarind juice.

"*Buen provecho,*" Escarlet said.

"*¡Buen provecho!*"

"*¡Buen provecho!*"

"Oh! Make sure you save room for dessert," Isabel said, pointing to the trays of pastries. "My aunt's *tres leches* is to die for!"

"*¿Tres leches?*" Sage asked, searching for a translation. "Three ... milks?"

"Yep, my Aunt Magdelena's. Trust me. You don't want to miss it."

The music softened, and the speaker squealed from microphone feedback. "*Familia y amigos,*" a man's voice echoed through the evening air. "I should try ... to speak ... *en inglés* ... *porque* ... we have *especial* visitors with us on this night." He motioned for Mr. and Mrs. Flores to approach. "Carmen, my sister. And Roberto, my brother-in-law. Come here, please."

Sage watched Isabel's parents greet the man as they arrived at the microphone. "*Los niños de Veracruz* ... children of Veracruz. *Roberto y Carmen Flores*, we welcome you home. On this especial night, we celebrate the day of birth for your daughter ... and my niece. *Los cumpleaños de Isabel.*"

The crowd erupted in cheers. "*¡Isabel! ¡Isabel! ¡Feliz cumpleaños!*"

Isabel's uncle scanned the crowd. "*¿Dónde estás, Isabel?*"

"*¡Aquí!*" She hopped in place while waving a hand in the air.

"*Hola, chula,*" he said. "You also are child of Veracruz. We carry you in the hearts and prayers for always."

Sage scanned the faces looking at her and Isabel. The raw compassion was completely unfamiliar. *This is a …* She searched for the appropriate word to describe the moment. *This is a … community.* Never before had she witnessed so many people participating in an event on behalf of loved ones. Never before had she felt so much togetherness, intimacy, and collective love. *This whole experience is just so*—she giggled at the ironic word she thought of next—*foreign.*

Isabel tapped her on the shoulder. "I'm happy you're here, Sage-asaurus. This has been the best birthday ever."

"Of course, Izzy-dactyl. I mean … *de nada.*"

"Watch out!" a voice shouted before a boy crashed to the ground in front of the girls. "*¡Buena patada, amigo!*" The boy hopped up, tossed a glance at Sage, and then returned to the impromptu soccer match.

The music faded into silence, and time slowed down as she watched the boy kick the ball through the crowd. She began to feel a bit lightheaded and wiped a sweaty palm against her shorts, trying to swallow despite a dry mouth.

"Hello? Earth to Sage." Isabel waved a hand in her face.

Sage's eyes fluttered as she returned to the moment. "Wha ... what'd you say, Izzy?"

Isabel pointed with her fork. "I said ... that's my cousin, Victor. Escarlet's big brother. He lives here with my aunt and uncle, too."

"You're kidding!"

"He's a year older than me ... so about fourteen now."

"Oh great," Sage said. "This *is* gonna be a long night."

"*Y ahora,*" Isabel's uncle continued. "The time arrives to sing to Isabel."

The audience roared. "*¡Sí! ¡Is-a-bel! ¡Is-a-bel!*"

"*Entonces,*" the man said. "*Uno, dos, tres ... ¡vamos!*"

The loving patrons serenaded Isabel with a Spanish-language rendition of the happy birthday tune. As the song concluded, Mr. and Mrs. Flores carried a small tray toward the girls, with a home-made cake featuring candles in the shape of a one and a three.

"Make a wish, *mi amor,*" Mrs. Flores said.

Isabel closed her eyes, muttered a few words, and blew out the candles. The flames disappeared ... then reappeared a moment later. Again, Isabel puffed them out ... and again they reappeared. Sage and Benji joined Isabel as the three kids continued blowing out the stubborn flames.

The partygoers howled at the sight of the struggling kids.

"Trick candles!" Isabel said with a laugh. "Good one, Mommy!"

The patrons applauded, and the party continued rocking.

As the crowd returned its attention to the festivities, a series of thoughts rushed through Sage's head. *We're running out of time! I mean, we found Frida's second cipher at the palace today, but we haven't solved it yet. Plus, we have only two more days in Mexico! What if we don't figure it out in time? We need to develop Izzy's pictures. We have to solve Frida's cipher!*

She squeezed Isabel's hand. "Hey, Izzy, I know we're in the middle of this great party and all, but I was thinking ... I mean I was wondering—"

Isabel jumped in. "We need to develop my pictures!"

Regardless of how often it happened, Sage was always amazed at how she and Isabel shared the same thoughts. "It's all I can think about."

"Me too! Come on." Isabel led Sage through the party. "My chemicals are inside. And we can use Victor's photo lab for processing."

As Benji trailed the girls—and Escarlet trailed Benji—the whole gang made their way inside the house.

13

Midnight Development

Sage stared intently as Isabel dipped the photo paper into various tubs of chemicals. The overhead light flooded the tiny room with an eerie red glow. Sage was packed inside—shoulder to shoulder—with Isabel, Benji, and Escarlet.

"Do you see anything yet? How do the pictures look?"

"Hold on, Benji," Isabel said. "We'll find out in a minute."

"Ow, my arm!"

"Shhh, Benji!"

"We need more space in here!"

"Watch it, that's my foot!" Sage said.

"Well, I have to stand somewhere," Benji replied, stumbling closer to Escarlet.

"You are going to tell what is this mystery?" Escarlet asked him. "Wow, you are *muy inteligente*, Benji."

"Call me *Benjamin*, please." He tried to lean

away from his admirer.

"Benji!" Sage shoved him back against Escarlet.

"Calm down, guys," Isabel said while continuing to process the film. "Just need a few more seconds, and then it's on to the fixer."

Sage watched Isabel focus on the task. She was a master at concentrating, and no task engrossed her like photography. Sage always believed that Isabel's hands were specially made to hold a camera.

Suddenly the room's door opened from the outside, and rays of fluorescent light entered. "The light!" Isabel shouted. "Close the door!"

"Door!"

"Shut it!"

Sage felt a fourth body scrunch inside as the door whipped closed. And in the dim red light, she found herself face to face with Victor.

"*¡Hola!*"

Sage's heart raced as she struggled for words. "*Hola.*"

"*Soy* Victor," he announced, as if the tiny room was a concert hall. "*¡Un placer!*"

Benji adjusted his glasses. "Hi, Victor! I'm Benjamin."

"Hi, nice to know you." He tapped Isabel on the shoulder. "*Hola, prima. ¡Feliz cumpleaños!*"

Isabel flashed him a smile. "*¡Gracias!*" She motioned with her head. "And that's Sage. *Ella es* *mi amiga mejor.*"

"Hi, Sage." Victor ran a hand through his hair. "It is a pleasure."

"Is there a fan in here by any chance, Izzy?" Sage waved a hand in front of her face. "Or maybe air conditioning?"

"Sorry, Sage-asaurus. No luck." Isabel giggled. "Think cold thoughts!"

"What is this you develop?" Victor asked. "Pictures of Mexico?"

"It's a cipher!" Benji proudly announced. "Frida's secret message!"

"Benji!"

He shrugged. "What, he's not our parents. It's cool."

Technically, he was right. Victor was just another one of the kids.

"What does this mean ... a cipher? *¿Qué quiere decir?*"

"Well," Sage said. "It's like a code ... a secret message."

Isabel nodded. "We found this one in the National Palace. In the Diego Rivera mural."

"*No me diga.*" Victor leaned in for a closer look at Isabel's workflow. "And do you believe this *cipher* has a significance?"

Sage thought of how to best respond to the question. To be completely honest, she hadn't the faintest idea exactly where Frida's cryptogram would ultimately lead them. However, she did know one thing without a doubt: The cryptogram *was* significant. "Yes," she said. "I do."

"And do you believe that you will *learn* this significance?" he asked. This was another great question, which forced her to think. She watched Isabel move the film from the developing liquid to a second tub with the word 'Fixer' scribbled on its side.

From the moment they discovered the first cipher in the Frida Kahlo museum yesterday, Sage had repeatedly asked herself the very same question: *Will we learn the significance?* Now she looked at Victor. He seemed fixated on Sage while awaiting her answer, much the same way that Isabel was currently focused on developing the film. He never broke eye contact until Sage responded.

"Yes," she said. "We'll learn the significance. We're going to solve the mystery."

He nodded and finally looked away. But this time it was Sage who stared at him. Her heartbeat quickened as small beads of sweat collected on her palms. She tugged on her shirt to allow cooler air to reach her skin. Victor looked once more at Sage, catching her in a direct gaze. She looked away. *Did he see me? Was I staring? This is so embarrassing.* She looked quickly at him to see if he was still looking at her. He wasn't. *Am I staring again? Oh no!*

Sage, stop looking at him! She noticed Victor's head turning toward her. *He's gonna look at me again. Sage, turn away!* She spun toward Isabel, and this time, turned her whole body so that Victor was behind her. *Oh great,* she thought. *Now I can't see Victor, but I can feel him looking at me. I hate that!*

"Done!" Isabel announced. "It's fixed."

Benji scrunched his face. "Fixed?"

"The final step in the development process." Isabel dipped the photo into another tub with 'Agua' printed on its side. "That's because the fixer ... um, well, it *fixes* the image to the paper. Otherwise, our oily fingers would smear the photo when we touched it."

"So, how do the photos look?"

"Great!" she said. "High ASA film. Sixteen hundred. Super-fast. I left the shutter open for about an eighth of a second. Handheld at 28 millimeters. Aperture was f/8, just because I needed depth of field. I wanted to make sure the whole scene was razor sharp. Plus, it's a good thing I shoot on film. During processing, I had to enlarge a specific part of the negative so that we could have a better view of Frida's message. I couldn't have done that with digital. Not enough resolution."

Sage understood little of what Isabel was saying, but she did remember her earlier critical thoughts about Isabel's use of film equipment. *Guess I was wrong,* she thought. *I sure am glad Izzy uses film!* "So you got the shot?" she asked.

"I got it, Sage-asaurus." Isabel fanned the damp photo in the air. "You can open the door now."

A latch clicked, and five bodies tumbled out with sighs of relief.

14

Cracking the Cipher

Sage stretched and took a deep breath as Isabel laid the enlarged print on the floor for everyone to see:

⬡ 0.33 | ♡ 1/3 | 3:5 △ 4 5/10.

9 5:10 0.2 2/6 6:10 5/15 0.5 ▢ 11/22 2:8 ♡ 8/20 0.6.

9 2:10 1/3 ⬜ 2:5 4 4/12 9 2:5 ▢ 0 20/30

▢ 0.5 4:8 3/5 0.75 | 15/30 9:15 0 0.2 2:3

1/2 3:5 7:14 0.25 0.75 20/30 □

0 0.4 7 1:3 1/2

30:50 15/20 2/5 4 8/12 △ 1:2

10/40 4 1 3:5 △ 1/3.

♡ 2/5 6:10 △ 4 0.5 2:5 12/20

0 8 1/2 □ 8 4/6

9 1:2 □ 0.33 ♡ □ 8 2/3 △

3/9 1/6 □.

3 2:4 0.25 1:3 2/12 0 8 9:18 4

10/15 ⬡ 2:3 □

5:10 10:50 9 50/100 0.6 0

2/3 0.25 3/18 10:15 ⬡ □ 3:15

3:5 2 1 2/3 0.2 △.

"Do you have your magnifying glass, Izzy?"

Isabel hopped over to her red backpack and retrieved a small magnifying glass, along with a flashlight. She handed Sage the magnifying glass then shined a beam of light onto the photograph.

Sage retrieved the *Book of Love*, flipped through to a clean page, and placed it beside the photo. "This is perfect," she said while writing dashes in the book. "Now we have the full cipher from the National Palace."

"Let's see ... which symbols do we already have?"

"Well, we know the square is S ... and we know 1/5 is F ... let's see, 10/15 is equivalent to 2/3, so that must be A."

Isabel leaned in. "Hexagon is Y. And 2:3 is another A."

Sage looked at Benji. "It's the same language as before. Frida's using math and geometry again."

Isabel pointed to the final blank lines in the journal. "Heart, star..." She slid her finger across the page to their key. "That's ... F, K."

Sage repeated the letters as her heart nearly leapt out of her chest. "Frida Kahlo!"

"Her signature!"

Benji shrugged. "Well, Mr. Ray said we should write our *full* names in the closing ... but I guess initials are okay."

Escarlet swooned. "*Que bonito*, Benjamin."

Sage dropped the pen and examined the deciphered message:

You found me.
Pero no es el fin.
Pro ⬜ ima pista se encuentra en el castillo encima del mundo.
Find me in the shapes of shadows.
Belo 2/12 the maya serpent al 3/18 ays on guard.
– F K

"We have some new symbols here."

"New ciphertext?"

"Yeah. They weren't in Frida's first message, so we never deciphered them."

"Two-twelfths," Isabel said. "And 3/18 ... they're equivalent! They both break down to 1/6."

"Great job, Izzy! So that means they're the same letter. This sentence looks like it's written in English ... B, E, L, O, *blank* ... Belo ..."

"Below!" Benji shouted. "*Below* the Maya serpent ..."

Sage inserted a W in the plaintext and added another W in the second blank.

You found me.

Pero no es el fin.

Pro △ ima pista se encuentra en el castillo encima del mundo.

Find me in the shapes of shadows.

Below the maya serpent always on guard.

- F K

"See?" Benji pointed to the plaintext. "'*Below* the Maya serpent *always* on guard'!"

Isabel gave him a high-five. "Great job, Benji-raptor!"

Escarlet placed her head on his shoulders. "*Mi principito.*"

"And look, we have a new shape," Sage said. "A trapezoid."

"Trapezoid?" Victor said. "This is a shape?"

"Sí, primo," Isabel said. "The one that looks kind of like … a *pyramid*. Well, a pyramid with its top chopped off."

"Like in *Palenque*," Victor said. "Or *Chichén Itzá*."

"Exactly."

"But what does it *mean*?" Benji asked. "What *letter* does the trapezoid represent?"

Sage tapped the pen against the paper. "This

132

sentence is in Spanish. 'Something … *pista se encuentro en el Castillo* … P, R, O, blank, I, M, A."

She looked to Isabel and Victor. "Any ideas, guys?

Victor sounded out the clue. "Pro … pro …"

Isabel twirled the photo for a better look while mumbling the phrase. "*En el castillo* … pro …

"*Próxima!*" Escarlet shouted. "*Próxima pista!*"

Sage looked to Isabel for confirmation.

Isabel read the sentence aloud. "*Próxima pista se encuentra* …" She nodded. "I think that's right!"

Sage wrote an X in the final blank:

You found me.

Pero no es el fin.

Proxima pista se encuentra en el castillo encima del mundo.

Find me in the shapes of shadows.

Below the maya serpent always on guard.

- F K

"But what does it *mean?*" Benji asked. "The *whole* message."

Sage giggled. "Well, the first sentence is easy. 'You found me.'"

Isabel translated the next two. "'But it is not the end … the next clue is located in the … castle on top of the world.'"

Sage finished the remaining English text. "'Find me in the shapes of shadows ... Below the Maya serpent always on guard ... Frida Kahlo.'"

"Aw, man!" Benji said. "You mean we have to find *another* clue? Why can't Frida just tell us whatever it is she wants us to know? For crying out loud, we only have—" He glanced at his watch. "—*Two* more days in Mexico. How are we supposed to solve anything if she keeps sending us on wild-goose chases all over the country?"

"Benji!" Sage motioned for him to lower his voice, though she shared his frustration. Their time was running out, and she knew it was possible that they wouldn't solve Frida's riddle before departing Mexico. She repeated the message. "Maya serpent always on guard, shapes and shadows ... the castle on top of the world. Any idea what it means, Izzy?"

Isabel repeated the code again but didn't seem to find any significance.

Victor waved a finger in the air. "*No es* 'the castle,' *prima*. It is ... *El Castillo*."

"And what's that?" Benji asked.

Escarlet leaned in. "*El Castillo, mi principito, ésta en Chichén Itzá. En Yucatán*."

"*El templo de Kukulkan*. It is very famous Maya temple in Mexico," Victor said.

"Maya!" Sage said, pointing to the same word in the plaintext. "*El Castillo ... Maya.*" She snapped her fingers. "That's it! That's the answer ... and our next clue."

"What?" Benji asked again.

Sage pointed out the window. "This temple in Chichen Itza. Frida's next clue for us is at ... *El Castillo!*"

Isabel hugged Sage. "I wonder if that's our *final* clue. I sure hope so!"

"Me too, Izzy."

"Do you travel to *Chichén Itzá* while you visit Mexico?" Victor again gazed intently at Sage. "Is *very* beautiful."

Sage blushed then responded. "We're going to *Yucatán* tomorrow." She grabbed Benji's wrist to look at his watch. "Well, actually *today*! I didn't realize how late it was."

"It's after midnight," Benji announced. "Our shuttle leaves in about four hours."

"No sleep for you!" Victor stood. "Come Escarlet, allow our friends to rest." But Escarlet remained focused on Benji. "*Hermana, ¡ven!*" He grabbed her arm and led her to the door. "We see you all in the morning. And, Sage, *un grande placer.*" He smiled. "*Buenas noches.*"

Benji hopped into bed. "*Buenas noches*, Victor."

Escarlet poked her head out from behind her

brother. *"Buenas noches, mi principito.* Goodnight, my prince. *Hasta mañana."*

Isabel trudged to her bunk. "Goodnight, everyone. *Buenas ..."*

Sage thought she heard Izzy snoring before her head even hit the pillow. *"Buenas noches,* Izzy. And Benji. Escarlet. And ... Victor. *Muchas gracias por todo.* We couldn't have done it without your help."

"De nada." He and Escarlet backed out of the room. *"Dulces sueños."* He closed the door.

"Tomorrow," Sage said to herself, already half-asleep. "We'll find Frida's next clue tomorrow at *El Castillo,* and after that, my SCUBA dive in Cozumel ..."

As she closed her eyes, her ears awakened to the soothing ocean sounds outside the window. While lying in bed, she envisioned the television commercials that advertised sleep aids: countless fluffy sheep leaping overhead in a dreamy thought-cloud. On this night, her brain overflowed with jumping fractions, ratios, and the occasional geometric shape. As she counted triangles and squares, a steady breeze whooshed outside, and the soft breaks of ocean waves rocked her to sleep.

15

In the Castle's Shadows

Isabel snapped several pictures of Sage as she stared at the glorious stone temple; sky-scraping forests filled the background, and a clear blue sky rested above. "Okay, your turn," she said as the girls swapped places.

Through the viewfinder, Sage composed Isabel's body in front of the enormous temple.

Click.

"Got it, Izzy!"

A piercing whistle broke the silence. The kids looked up, searching for its source. Gazing into the harsh sun, Sage saw the silhouettes of two monkeys standing atop a nearby monument.

"Howler monkeys!" Isabel said. "They're super cute!"

The animals hollered once more, then scooted across the stone platform and leapt into nearby trees. They disappeared into the dense forest canopy, their wails trailing into the distance.

Sage examined the stone platform and noticed a series of steps ascending to the top. "Let's go up there!" she said. "Let's climb it!"

As they approached the temple, she saw a massive stone head carved into the base; it looked like a giant hissing snake. She shifted her attention to the top of the temple. "'The castle on top of the world ... find me in the shapes and shadows.'" She pointed to the top. "Our next clue's up there, guys."

Isabel snapped several pictures then climbed the first step. "Let's go!"

"Careful, Izzy. Take your time, Benji." Sage scaled the second step. Then the third. The fifth. Seventh. She trailed Benji, watching his every move. "Good, Benji. That's it." As he struggled a bit, she rushed over to assist.

"Are we there yet?" Finally, his face rose above the final step. He slung a leg up, gripped the surface, and hoisted his body.

"We're here!" Isabel announced.

"We did it!" Benji added.

Sage wiped her forehead and scanned the valley below. "We just climbed the Castle."

"*¡El Castillo!*"

The kids stood back to back, and Sage took in the 360-degree view of the surroundings. Visibility was limitless, and she reveled in the vast expanse of dense forest all around. "Just look at all these trees. They're absolutely amazing." She noticed Isabel fixating on the temple's steep stone staircase and tried to follow her line of sight to see what her best friend was looking at. "What is it, Izzy?"

"It's just ..." Isabel tilted her head. "The shadows ..."

Sage felt a breeze tickle her neck, and as the forest's sounds diminished, she entered a moment of tranquility. The eerie silence seemed to enhance what she saw while gazing down the Castle's staircase. She knelt for a better view, and the warm stone sent a pulse of heat radiating through her body. Her heart beat steadily faster, and her breaths were shorter as she stared at a collection of shadows on the staircase. *What are those?*

"The shapes," Isabel finally spoke. "Square. Triangle. Oval." She knelt to the ground next to Sage. "Do you see them?"

Sage scanned the temple in search of the source of these perfect geometric shadows. But she saw no triangular or oval details in the pyramid's construction.

Isabel retrieved the *Book of Love* from her backpack, flipped several pages, and began reading. "The next clue is located in the castle on top of the world. Find me in the shapes of shadows ... below the Maya serpent always on guard."

"Below the Maya serpent always on guard," Benji repeated. "Serpent ... that's like a snake, right?"

"Shapes in shadows ... a castle on top of the world." Sage spun in place, examining every detail of the temple's summit. "A Maya serpent always on guard."

"Are you sure *this* is the castle on top of the world?" Benji cleaned his glasses. "Maybe Frida's talking about someplace else. I betcha there's lots of castles in Mexico."

"No, this is it," Sage said. "I just ... *feel* it. We're in the right place." She continued investigating every crack and crevasse in sight. "Shadows," she said while turning her attention to the distant forests; the dense trees formed green walls of foliage. "Trees, forests ... *shadows*." She tried to trigger something—anything—to solve Frida's mystery. "Shapes, squares, triangles, circles, polygons ..." She reached, but nothing came to mind. *Think, Sage!*

"Nefertari Sage Carrington!" her mom's voice boomed from below.

Uh oh! My full name. Mom's serious!

"We have to go," Benji said, pointing to the valley. "The van's here. Everyone's getting inside!" He began down the steps.

"Isabel Carmen Flores!" Mrs. Flores shouted. "*Now*, young lady!"

Sage and Isabel looked at each other. They both knew the clock was ticking; they also knew the next clue in Frida's cryptogram was right under their noses. But what was it? *Where* was it?

Isabel opened her mouth to speak, but no words came out. Sage understood; what else was there to say?

Mrs. Carrington yelled from the valley below. "Sage, time to go!"

"Just a minute, Mom!"

"Isabel!" Mrs. Flores added. "Come on!"

Isabel tightened the straps on her backpack and looked at Sage. "We're so close!"

Sage gazed into the sky. "If you're with us—if you're here—we need help, Frida."

Their mothers yelled together. "Let's go. Now!"

Sage's heart sank as she began down the temple. *This can't be how it ends. I promised Frida we'd solve her puzzle. And I can't give up until we do.* She stepped into the various shadows peppering the stones: circles, squares, and triangles. Then she froze mid-step. "Izzy!" She pointed to the statue at the base of the temple. "*Snake!*"

"Snake!" Isabel leapt into the air, terrified. "Where!?"

"No, not a *real* snake, Izzy. Frida said the serpent was 'always on guard.' That's because it's a *stone statue*! Get your camera ready, Izzy-dactyl.

We only have a minute to get some pictures." *This has to be it,* she thought. "Frida's next clue isn't *on top* of the Castle." She hopped down another step. "It's *under* the snake's head." She watched Benji descend the final step, then race across the grounds toward the idling van. The vehicle's open door gave Sage a clear view of her irritated mother. "One second, Mommy! We're coming!"

The girls hurried down the final steps and set foot on the valley floor. Isabel started snapping pictures as Sage tiptoed around the snake's head and examined every inch. She noticed the intricate stonework of the eyes and scaly skin. "Where are you?" she said. "I know the clue's here." She heard the click of Isabel's camera as she kneeled to the ground, poked her head inside the snake's open mouth, and peered into its throat. Suddenly she spotted something. It was different ... not stone but rather...

... "I found it!" she shouted at the sight of the metal plaque. "This is it!"

Isabel joined Sage inside the serpent's mouth. "I need to drag the shutter for more ambient light," Isabel said. "It's kind of dark in here."

"Sage!" Mr. Carrington shouted from across the valley. "Now!"

"More numbers," Sage reached into Isabel's backpack for a pen and paper. She jotted the digits onto the paper before turning to race to the van. After a few steps, she realized that she had left Isabel behind. She trotted back to the temple and tugged on Isabel's backpack. "We have to go!"

Isabel fired off a few more frames.

"Izzy, we have to get into the van. Don't worry. I got it!"

Isabel started backpedaling, still snapping pictures of the temple before Sage spun her around and sent the girls into an all-out dash across the valley floor.

As they neared the vehicle, Sage paused for one final view of Chichen Itza—the crown jewel of ancient Mayan civilization. The jungle. The valley. The monuments. Her thoughts returned to the serpent's head. *It's the next piece of Frida's puzzle! Now we have another cryptogram to decipher. But first ...* She turned and shouted to Isabel as they arrived at the van. "It's SCUBA time!"

"Cozumel!" Isabel said.

"¡*Vamos!*" The girls hopped inside to the sound of grumbling parents. The vehicle's engine roared to life as the team departed for Mexico's Caribbean coast.

16

Constant Change

Sage and Isabel sat at the end of a pier, their feet dangling below them. Jet skiers raced across the horizon, followed by roaring speedboats. The coastline overflowed with beachgoers swimming and bathing in the afternoon sun. A group of friends played volleyball in the surf. One player leapt and—

Pow!

He spiked the ball to the ground. His opponent ate a face-full of sand while diving to save the point. The ball bounced off the player's arms, shot into the nearby tide, and a girl dashed into the water to retrieve it. While returning to the game, she passed a sign: *Cozumel Diving Center*.

"Izzy, you should at least try it," Sage said. "Just thirty minutes. You'd love it."

Isabel stood. "I—I don't think so, Sage-asaurus. Not this time."

"It's amazing out there. Well ..." Sage pointed to

the water. "*Down* there."

Isabel seemed like she wanted to change the subject. "So anyway … what do you think Frida's latest cipher means?" She reached into her backpack, retrieved the *Book of Love*, and flipped through the journal. She arrived at the page with "Frida's Cryptogram from Chichen Itza" scribbled across its top. The page was full of familiar geometric shapes and math symbols. Beneath the cipher, Sage read the decrypted message from Frida:

Look again for the first time.
Find me in the light.
- F K

"I've been thinking about it, Izzy. But I'm stumped. What about you?"

"Stumped to the tenth power, Sage-asaurus."

Drusilla strolled down the pier and joined the girls. "*¡Buenas tardes!*"

"Hey, Aunt Dru!"

"Hi, Mrs. Dru!"

"What are you girls doing?"

"Just getting some fresh air."

Drusilla wrapped an arm around Isabel. "You joining Sage on the underwater SCUBA adventure?"

Isabel giggled nervously. "Not today, Mrs. Dru."

"You don't know what you're missing," Sage said.

"Isabel!" Mrs. Flores called from farther down the shore. "Let's go!"

Isabel tapped her backpack. "I'm gonna take a photo walk with my mom while you're out there exploring the deep blue sea. I'll have the chance to use my vintage 200 millimeter lens. Super excited!"

Sage waved at Isabel's mom. "Hi, Mrs. Flores!"

"Hi, love!" she shouted. "Good luck down there! Isabel, *vamanos!*"

"I've gotta go. But first ... hey, Sage ..." Isabel raised her camera. "Say, cheeeeeseburger!"

"Cheeeeeseburger!"

Click. Click.

Isabel gave a thumbs up. "*Buena suerte*, Sage-asaurus. *Cuidado!*"

"Thanks, Izzy. I'll be careful. Promise." They hugged.

"See you later, Mrs. Dru."

"Of course, dear." They also hugged. "Have a great photo walk."

Isabel jogged down the pier, waving. "Thanks, I will!"

Drusilla sat on the pier beside Sage, her feet dangling above the water as well. "Well, Bird, you sure have a beautiful day for diving. I've never seen such blue skies and clear water."

Sage's mind remained on last week's incident at Aunt Drusilla's award ceremony. She had tons of questions and desperately wanted answers. *How come Aunt Dru never told me she was so sick? That's a big secret to keep from me! And what's going to happen to her now?* "Aunt Dru, how come you didn't tell me your cancer mastasized?"

"Yeah." Drusilla exhaled deeply. She seemed to have known that this conversation was coming. "Well, first of all, Bird, it's *metastasized*." She nodded. "I should have told you about the leukemia. About my cancer. How it came back. And how it's spread."

"So why didn't you tell me? It's not fair because I tell you *everything*."

"I was scared, Bird. Plus, I just didn't want you to worry."

"I'm twelve, Aunt Dru ... almost thirteen. I can handle it!"

"I know, sweetie."

"You always say, 'Bird, tell the whole truth.' Like the time I smashed that beaker in your lab then swept up the glass and tossed it into the trash without telling you. Or when I accidentally mixed some of your dry ice with the hot water and those two security guards came rushing in after seeing all the smoke. I mean *really*, it was just an itsy bitsy explosion. Nothing major."

Drusilla looked surprised. "You 'accidentally' created a smoke bomb in my lab? I don't recall hearing about that."

"Oh," Sage said with shifty eyes. "Well, you know, we didn't want you to worry. Besides, it really wasn't a big deal, Aunt Dru. Honest."

"Hmmm. Broken beakers, lab experiments ... it looks like you *also* have a few secrets, Bird."

Sage realized Aunt Dru was right. *I've kept some things from her too.* She also noticed how pleasant Aunt Dru seemed after hearing these revelations. *She's not even upset, like I was with her.* "I'm sorry."

"No need to apologize, sweetie. Everyone has secrets. Some are bigger than others. As for me, I don't want my health issues to remain hidden from you anymore." She held Sage's hands. "I have leukemia, Bird. It's a form of cancer that inhabits my bones and my blood. And it's very difficult to cure."

I can't ask her. But I have to know. I just don't want to say it! Sage felt tears filling her eyes. "Does that mean that you ... that you're going to ..." She hugged Drusilla. *I can't even finish the sentence!*

Drusilla patted Sage's back. "That's a normal thought and a fair question to ask." She released Sage, then wiped her eyes. "The doctors are considering every option. Blood transfusions, chemotherapy, maybe even a bone-marrow transplant."

Sage didn't understand any of the treatment options her aunt was describing, but they all sounded very serious. "So the doctors can cure your leukemia?"

"They'll do everything in their power, but as is the case with everything in life, nothing's guaranteed." As Sage lowered her chin, Drusilla lifted it. "I promise you this, Bird. I'm fighting every single day. And I'll be waiting right here for you to return. I'm not going anywhere. Okay?"

This is a good time to ask Aunt Dru ... but how? I want to tell her what's going on with my body, too ... it's just so embarrassing. But I can talk to Aunt Dru about anything, and she'd never laugh or make fun of me. "Aunt Dru, why does my body have to change—I mean ... why do *our* bodies have to change?" *Awww shoot, I accidentally told her, but I didn't mean to say it exactly like that!* "Why can't *our* bodies just ... stay the same?"

Drusilla seemed to grasp Sage's hints, since her facial expression shifted to one of great discovery. "Of course. *That's* what this is all about. You're twelve years old ..."

"I'll be thirteen next week. But now, with how strange everything is feeling inside, I just ... I'm not sure I want to become a teenager. I want to stay twelve for a while longer. That way I'll never be thirteen ... or thirty. Then my body won't feel so

149

crazy. And I'll never grow old and maybe get s—"

"You can say it. Get *sick*?"

"I didn't mean it like that, Aunt Dru. I promise!"

Drusilla smiled. "It's okay, sweetie. I know exactly how you feel."

"You do?"

"I realize this might be hard to believe, Bird, but I was once a twelve-year-old girl myself. Come here." She wrapped an arm around Sage. "One of the hardest things to deal with in life is change. And I don't care if you're twelve ... or one hundred. Just about everyone's afraid of change. Because it's the *unknown*. We're all so comfortable in our current thoughts and behaviors. But if we change, then what will we feel? How will we think? What will happen in the future?"

"Yes! So, you understand? I feel so different, Aunt Dru. Everything's moving around inside ... and it's scary." Victor's smiling face flashed across Sage's mind. "Things I've never thought and feelings I've never felt before."

"Ah, yes, I remember like it was yesterday. Riverside Junior High. We sat next to each other in Mr. Sterdavant's history class." She leaned in. "His name was Bobby Stewart."

Sage gasped. *How did she know I was talking about a boy!?* Then she chuckled. "Bobby Stewart?"

"He was the most handsome boy in school ...

well, in *my* opinion anyway. I couldn't even look at him. I'd get these butterflies in my stomach, and the words in my brain would scramble. It was awful!"

Sage laughed. "Yeah, what's *that* all about, anyway?"

"It's nature, dear." She examined the colorful bracelet on Sage's wrist. "I sat next to Bobby for nine months, and I maybe said three words to him the whole time. I was terrified!"

"Last year I didn't even care about boys, but now ... I *do*! And it's how you said ... all these funny feelings inside. Like last week on the baseball field with Germ ... and it happened again yesterday when I met Victor—"

"Victor?" Drusilla appeared to search her memory. "The boy from Isabel's party?

Sage blushed and nodded. "This is so embarrassing."

"You have good taste, Bird!"

"Aunt Dru!" She rested her head on Drusilla's arm. "I just don't know what to say ... or how to act."

"Just be yourself, dear. That's all anyone can do. And when you're at a loss for words, try to remember this one: *hi*. You'd be amazed how far those two letters can get you!"

"Aunt Dru, how long will I ... *feel* like this? I mean, is it like when I catch a cold and then I'm better a few days later? I just want to get back to my old self again."

"Well it doesn't work exactly like that, Bird."

"But what if I don't want to be an adult? I'm not done being a kid yet. I'm just ... I'm not ready."

"It's all very confusing and difficult." She gazed into the sea. "Lord knows it was for me."

"Really? You too?"

"Absolutely." Drusilla smiled. "By the way, have you talked to your mom?"

"Yeah. She tells me it's normal and that every girl goes through it. But I just wanted to know what *you* thought about everything."

"Well, now you know." Drusilla ran a hand across Sage's head. "Look at this beautiful hair."

"Thank you."

"You shouldn't be embarrassed or feel like every-thing has to be a secret. When you're trying to fig-ure things out, talk to me or your parents. We've all been there ... done that."

"I understand."

"My grandma used to tell me, 'Sunlight is the best disinfectant.'"

"What's that mean?"

"It means share what's on your mind, Bird. No need to keep *everything* secret."

"'Sunlight is the best disinfectant,'" Sage repeated.

"You had more bouncing around inside that

brain than I thought!"

Sage nodded.

"Nothing stays the same forever, babe. The only constant in life is change. Understanding—and accepting—this fact is one of the thresholds that distinguishes children from adults."

"What's a threshold?"

"It's a line in the sand that must be crossed before the next phase in a process can occur. And once it's crossed, the sand blows away, and that previous phase is gone forever."

"It's so unfair."

Just then, a barefoot man strutted down the pier. His tanned chest revealed a trim, athletic physique. Immediately behind the shirtless man was a young woman. Both carried orange duffel bags.

"*¡Buenas tardes!*" the man said. "You must be Sage."

17

Abril and Fernando

"*¡Buenas tardes!* Yep, that's me!" They shook hands.

"My name is Fernando, and this is my wife, Abril."

"*Mucho gusto.*" Sage pointed to Abril. "I love your bathing suit."

"Thank you." Abril looked at Fernando. "She's too sweet!"

"We are your Divemasters today," Fernando said. "You are in—how do you say—good hands? For we have specialization in deep dives and search and recovery. Have no fear. We are the two best divers in all of Quintana Roo."

"This is not entirely true," Abril said. "Actually, my husband wants to say ... in all of *Mexico*."

Fernando shrugged. "Who am I to argue with such a beautiful woman?"

Sage laughed at the couple's loving banter. "And

you both dive for the Smithsonian too. I did my homework."

"Sweet *and* smart," Abril said. "A magnificent combination." She began prepping the boat for departure. "You are correct, Sage. We are divers for the International Consortium. We explore underwater ruins and deep-sea shipwrecks."

"Cooool!"

"And with us, Sage, you are family. We know your parents for fifteen years."

Fernando gazed into the distance. "We have a clear day. Great visibility—forty meters. Do you dive alone today, Sage?"

Sage glanced at Aunt Drusilla.

"Don't look at me, Bird! This body wasn't built for SCUBA!"

"Yes, it's just me, Fernando."

"Are you excited?" Abril asked. "This is for certificación?"

"Super excited!" Sage said. "I finished the coursework and training in the United States. I already had four dives at a SCUBA center back home in Washington. So this is the final dive to earn my Open Water!"

Drusilla held Sage's shoulders. "Your mom and dad are in a conference for a few more hours, and I promised them I'd look after you." She ran a hand through Sage's long, curly hair. "You know, with all the time you've spent in the water this year—swimming, surfing, SCUBA diving—maybe I should change your nickname from 'Bird' to 'Fish.'" She hugged Sage. "You be safe out there, okay? I love you."

Sage grasped her aunt's worried tone. "I will, Aunt Dru. And I love you too."

Fernando started the engine, and a puff of smoke billowed into the sky. Abril kicked her foot against the dock, sending the boat drifting into the current.

"Good luck, Bird!"

As the boat's motor purred to life, Sage smiled and blew kisses to Drusilla.

"Hold on to your seat," Fernando said before throttling forward. "And secure the life jacket, please."

The engine's soft purr grew into a steady roar, and Sage buckled the clips on her life preserver as the motorboat raced into an endless blue horizon.

18

Journey to the Aquarium

The boat sped across the open waters of the Caribbean, salt water spraying into Sage's face. She closed her eyes and smiled at the sensation of the warm droplets kissing her cheeks.

Abril stood up. "I am your Divemaster today, Sage. We are going to a site called '*El Aquarium*' this morning. The Aquarium. It holds more underwater life than your biggest dreams."

"The Aquarium?" Sage's face lit up. "That sounds incredible."

"It is," Fernando said from the steering wheel. "One of our favorite dives in all the world." He pointed into the distance. "Many people do not know, but this is the *second* largest coral reef formation in the world. Right here."

Abril looked at Sage. "Do you know the *first* biggest?"

Ever since Sage was a toddler, she'd been

fascinated by the largest reef system on the planet. And one day, she knew that she'd have a chance to go and visit. "In Australia," she responded. "The Great Barrier Reef."

Abril turned to Fernando. "She's a smart *chica*."

"Coral is the largest living organism on Earth," Fernando said. "And you will visit in a few minutes." He flashed a thumbs-up, then returned his attention to the boat's navigation.

Abril looked at the water, then at an enormous watch strapped to her wrist. "We will reach our destination in three minutes. Where is your BCD?"

Sage recalled the training videos she'd watched as part of her SCUBA coursework back home. She learned how the vest had chambers inside of it, which connected to the oxygen tank on her back. The vest's chambers could be inflated with air, allowing her to rise more easily to the surface of the sea. Alternatively, she could also release air from the vest, causing her to sink lower beneath the surface. She remembered the term for this ability to sink or float: buoyancy. She also remembered the name of the vest: buoyancy control device or BCD.

Sage pointed across the boat. "It's under the seat, Abril, with my mask and fins."

"Please put on your gear." Sage began attaching fins to her feet as Abril continued, "We will dive at ten meters for forty minutes." She scooted closer as

Fernando throttled down the engine. "As always, Sage, we'll have a three-minute safety stop at five meters. Fernando remains on the boat. He is here to help you get in and out of the water."

"Your safety is our first job." Fernando smiled. "We protect you." His cool, confident tone eased Sage's nerves a bit.

Abril slid into her fins. "While inside of The Aquarium, we may explore The Tunnel. It is a shallow cave full of adventure. What do you think?"

Sage nodded. "Absolutely!"

"Okay, then, we will do it." Abril reached a hand toward Sage's mask. "How does it feel? Fitting with comfort?"

"Yep, feels great."

"We enter the water with giant stride method," Abril said. "You have done this before?"

Sage nodded. "Once."

"Great, then you remember to find your BCD, lay on your back, and secure your equipment. And after it is secured on your body—" Abril held a closed fist atop her head. "—You give me the 'okay' sign. Right?"

Sage imitated Abril by placing a closed fist atop her head. "Right."

"Well then," Abril said as Fernando cut off the motor. The boat drifted atop the calm Caribbean water. "It is time. *Vamos, mi amor.*"

Fernando hopped down and trotted to the back of the boat. He lifted a buoyancy control device, along with its attached harnesses. "Ready, Sage?" She nodded, and he tossed the equipment into the water. "There's your BCD."

Sage waddled to the back of the boat and sat on a small bench. Abril scooted across to join her.

"One hand on your mask," Abril said, moving Sage's hand. "And the other here." She placed Sage's other hand on the back of her head. "Excellent. Now take a big step off the boat."

Before jumping in, Sage stared into the clear water below. From the boat, she could already see the coral beneath the water's wavy surface. Schools of fish teemed everywhere. A rainbow of life awaited her, and the sheer thought of her upcoming experience sent a surge of energy through her body. *I can't believe it. I'm going to dive the Caribbean!* She located the buoyancy control device floating beside the boat, and thought, *let's do it!* Then she extended a leg, hopped off, and splashed into the sea.

19

10,000 Millimeters Under the Sea

As muffled underwater sounds filled her head, Sage caught a brief glimpse of the sea life before bobbing to the surface. She was initially surprised at how warm the water was. Her legs and arms basked in the sea's soothing heat, and gobs of underwater bubbles tickled her skin. She took several deep breaths and readjusted her mask. Seawater streamed from her thick hair, trickled down her face, and even slipped past her lips into her mouth. The water's strong, salty smell was complemented by an equally intense taste.

"Okay, now find your buoyancy control device," Abril said from the boat. "Relax, Sage. Take your time."

Sage turned onto her backside and paddled to her BCD. She reached both arms through the vest's straps, thinking that it was just like putting on a book bag—well, if attaching a book bag involved floating on your back in the middle of the Caribbean Sea.

Abril kept a close eye on Sage. "Magnificent job, *mi amor*. Now close the straps and give me the signal."

Sage secured a strip of Velcro across her chest, fastened a few clips, and then closed a fist above her head. "All good," she said.

"Fantastic!" Abril replied.

"Yes, Sage," said Fernando. "Really excellent." He tossed a second set of equipment into the water.

Abril kissed Fernando then turned to Sage. "Here I come!"

Splash!

Abril attached her BCD and swam over. "I track our depth and time." She pressed a few buttons on her oversized wristwatch. "How is your air?"

Sage reached an arm into the water and retrieved a long tube with a circular gauge attached to its end. She examined the numbers on the face. "I'm at three thousand."

"Wonderful. Let us practice your breathing."

Sage placed the respirator into her mouth and inhaled deeply. She held a thumbs up as Abril pulled a second respirator from Sage's vest and breathed into it.

"Everything looks good." Abril performed the same tests on her own equipment, and indicated for

Sage to grab a tube on her vest. Sage complied and took several breaths from the alternate respirator attached to Abril's tank.

"Safety check is over." Abril removed her goggles and rinsed them in the seawater. "Remember, Sage. Long, slow breaths. This is not a race. We take our time and enjoy the ride."

Sage nodded. "Sounds perfect."

"Okay, so you are ready?" Abril replaced her goggles. "Breathe slowly."

Sage's mind raced as she imagined the upcoming experience. *But, how can I stay calm during the most amazing experience of my life?!*

Abril held a hand in the air, and Sage did the same. Then they both pressed a button on their buoyancy control devices and began to descend.

Sage watched the blue sky give way to a green sea. She continued pressing the button while keeping a close eye on Abril. Her instructor looked up every few seconds, to ensure that Sage was safe, and held her fingers together in the shape of an 'okay' sign. Sage nodded and mimicked the hand gesture.

While descending, Sage glanced up and noticed her air bubbles escaping to the water's surface with each breath. Next to the stream of bubbles, she saw a shard of sunlight cutting across the water's surface. After a few seconds, she realized, *I'm in the*

Caribbean. She took a long, deep breath and exhaled. *I'm actually DIVING IN THE CARIBBEAN!*

Her buoyancy control device burped a pocket of bubbles, which gurgled to the surface. She watched them float higher before turning her attention to the sea floor below. She lay weightlessly in a horizontal position, her dangling arms resting inches above the coral, and recalled Abril's voice: *We will dive to ten meters.* Sage loved to play with numbers; her vibrant mind quickly converted their depth into other units of measurement. *Ten meters is about 33 feet...one thousand centimeters ... or ten thousand millimeters. Wow!*

A group of excited fish zipped in front of her face, then between her arms and legs in an aquatic game of hide and seek. She felt herself drifting lower as Abril pointed to her chest and indicated for her to press a valve on the buoyancy control device. Sage gave the device a couple of quick bursts and felt the BCD inflating against her chest. Her depth stabilized, and she gave Abril the 'okay' sign.

Abril mimicked the gesture then followed it with a thumbs-up.

Suspended weightlessly, Sage was finally free to observe the world of the Caribbean Sea, thirty-three feet beneath its surface. All the weeks of coursework in Washington, DC—the tests, the training videos, and the long flight to Mexico. At last, her time had arrived. Finally, her dream was coming true.

She slowed her breathing and fully opened her eyes. The textures and colors were unlike anything she had ever witnessed before. The underwater environment just seemed so ... different. So vivid. Perhaps it was the way sunlight seemed to intensify after entering the sea, like a huge light box. Or perhaps it was the hypnotic back-and-forth movement of the coral that sent Sage into a relaxed trance as she watched the fish, crabs, lobsters, and other sea life prancing about. She imagined that some of the creatures were there to eat, while others were there to sleep. Regardless of the reasons, all thrived within the colossal reef system.

She remembered the aquarium in her classroom at school. The small tank housed a collection of tropical fish, a tiny treasure chest, and a plastic SCUBA diver. *Now I'm inside the aquarium,* she thought. *But this one doesn't have any glass sides.* She gazed into an endless blue expanse. *There's no limit.*

Click, click, click.

Sage spun in the direction of the sound. Abril was banging a metallic ring against her air tank to draw Sage's attention. She straightened her hand, fingers together, and placed it above her head like a fin. Sage knew this hand signal. *A shark!* She exhaled, sending a cloud of bubbles to the water's surface.

Abril glided to the bottom and wrapped both arms around a shark, then motioned for Sage to come closer. Abril rolled the shark onto its back as Sage extended a hand and stroked the underside of the fish. The feel of its sandpaper-like tummy sent another cloud of bubbles streaming from Sage's respirator. *I'm touching a shark,* she thought. *Wait 'til Isabel and Benji hear about this!*

The shark wiggled, and Abril released her grip. The fish flipped over and swam away.

Abril held up the 'okay' sign again. Sage mimicked the gesture then followed her instructor farther. Her head was on a swivel. The lively yellows. The deep blues. She had only witnessed reds like these in her dreams. Her certification dives back home were in a swimming pool. This Caribbean voyage was a completely different experience.

Click, click, click.

Abril tapped the metal ring on her tank again, then gestured with both fists together, thumbs twirling in circles. Sage floated closer to Abril and saw an enormous sea turtle approaching in the distance. The animal was bigger than Sage. The turtle swam past the divers—turning its head to look at the visiting humans—then calmly glided into the open blue.

Sage had never seen such an elegant animal, such a graceful swimmer. *This is unbelievable!* She continued following Abril toward a rock formation; a beam of sunlight shined through a hole in the rock's center. *This must be The Tunnel.* As they approached the entryway, Sage saw two lobsters camping out, their antennae spanning several feet.

Abril tapped two fingers onto the underside of her wrist, then pointed at Sage's oxygen tank. Sage understood the signal to check her air levels. She reached for the gauge; its needle firmly pointed to two thousand. Sage tapped two fingers against her wrist. Abril nodded and turned toward the cave.

Okay, Sage thought. *I can see daylight in there.* She felt relieved to know the tunnel opened up on the other side. In the shards of speckled light, a universe of suspended particles appeared in the water ahead. She recalled the time Benji had dipped an old mayonnaise jar into the Potomac River then shined a flashlight through the container, illuminating the millions of organisms living in it. *This is kind of the same, right? Except now I'm in the mayo jar too!*

She followed Abril's silhouette as they entered the tunnel. The cave was larger than she had previously thought. In fact, she spread her arms apart and couldn't even touch both sides. She examined her surroundings and noticed several smaller caves opening up on either side, like branches on a tree. In the fragmented light, the unique texture of the tunnel's stonework grabbed her attention. As she floated closer to the wall, she realized the textures weren't just random natural markings, but rather human writings. *What is this?* She ran her fingers across several messages etched into the stone. *Amanda y Miguel para siempre ... Me encanta a Juan ... El amor de Carol y Cristobal. They're ... love notes!*

Click, click, click.

She recognized Abril's call by now and backed away from the wall to make her way deeper into the tunnel. She turned a corner and froze at the sight of a massive ray gliding around Abril. White, circular spots accentuated the animal's dark body. It dove to the coral then ascended to the surface. Sage noticed the animal's light underbelly and what appeared to be a mouth. She could've sworn she saw the ray smiling at her.

Click, click, click.

Abril pointed into the blue expanse as two more rays joined the fray. The three animals encircled them like the featured act of a circus. As Sage and Abril continued forward, the three rays coasted right alongside them. The five swimmers glided across the coral, completely synchronized, completely calm.

Abril pointed to Sage's air tank and tapped a couple of fingers on her wrist. At the prompt, Sage reached for her air gauge again and saw the needle resting just above five hundred. Sage extended a hand in front of her body and spread apart all five fingers. Abril nodded then directed Sage to follow behind.

They began to slowly ascend, leaving the three rays behind. Sage watched Abril climb steadily higher before stopping a few feet short of the water's surface. As Sage caught up, Abril tapped her wristwatch then extended a few fingers. *Three minutes,* Sage thought. *A safety stop.* Sage remembered the importance of the safety stop before emerging; this was to ensure that her body adjusted to the lower pressure of the shallow depth before returning to the surface.

They stayed there, floating, until Abril finally held up a single finger. One more minute. She extended an arm and motioned across the coral to remind Sage to take a final look.

As instructed, Sage gazed into the distance once more. *All of these animals, plants, textures, and colors. And this feeling—the feeling of diving into the ocean … of breathing underwater. It's a different world down here. Like nothing else on earth.* Schools of fish swam around her; by now, they were fully comfortable with her presence in their space.

How can I even begin to describe all of this to Isabel? Well, I know one thing for sure: Izzy's diving with me next time. I won't take 'no' for an answer. She looked up and stared directly into the glimmering sun. She then saw the shadow of a boat floating into view.

Click, click, click.

Abril pointed to the surface and indicated for Sage to deflate her BCD. Sage complied then mightily kicked her legs. She looked up as the sunlight grew brighter, and finally her face emerged from the water's surface.

20

A Breath of Fresh Air

The Caribbean air rushed against her drenched face. Sounds returned—the wind, squawking birds, rippling water. Then she heard Fernando's voice.

"So? How was it?"

Sage lowered her goggles and located the boat. "Incredible!"

"How are you, Sage?" Abril asked.

Sage placed a closed fist atop her head, indicating she was fine. "Did you see the lobsters, Abril? And the sea turtle! And the clown fish. They're so cute! Oh, and Fernando, we swam with rays!"

"Spotted," Abril added.

"And I saw love letters! All along the walls of the tunnel. These short messages."

"Ah yes," Abril nodded, "I wanted to show you before, but I saw the rays, and they took my attention."

Fernando handed Sage a towel. "Many people

171

enter The Tunnel to write their name and a message of love, which remains eternally under the waters of Mexico. Sometimes we call this *el tunel del amor*."

"The Tunnel of Love," Sage said.

"I am happy you were able to see the love notes," Abril said. "Because this is the best time of the day for sunlight to reach into the tunnel."

"I'm happy too."

"It is all about perspective. I believe you say *timing* ... and the angle of the light."

The angle of the light echoed in Sage's mind as she thought about Frida's latest clue. *Find me in the light ...*

"*Vamos, mi niña.*" Fernando motioned for Sage to swim closer. "Let's get you on the boat."

Sage floated past Abril and reached for the ladder. Fernando grabbed hold of Sage's air tank and hoisted her up. They unstrapped the equipment, and Sage plopped down onto the seat. Water droplets streamed down her face as she enjoyed the view. She took several deep breaths, filling her lungs completely with fresh air.

The clear Caribbean sky rested atop the wavy sea surface, and Sage returned her attention to the water, its choppy surface making it appear like the reef was dancing below. *I was down there,* she thought. *I. Was. Down. There!*

"Well, Sage," Abril said, holding her hand up for a high-five. "You did it."

Sage hopped up and slapped Abril's hand. "I did it!"

"A forty-minute dive. *Muy bien, mi niña.*" Abril wrung a river of water from her hair. "Time moves fast down there, huh?"

"Forty minutes?" Sage said in disbelief. "Felt more like five."

Fernando nodded. "It always does." He opened a cooler and handed Sage a sandwich and a water bottle. He tossed the same to Abril.

Sage ripped open the plastic and began chomping on the sandwich. "Abril? What kind of shark was that?"

Abril took a moment to chew her food. "Nurse shark, *mi amor.* Always friendly."

"We have reef sharks around here too," Fernando said.

Abril sipped her water. "They are all friendly."

Sage took another bite then leaned over the side of the boat. She scanned the water. Afternoon sunlight sparkled off its surface. *Mexico is so beautiful.*

"We must return now, to your family and friends. You have a long night ahead, *mi niña.*"

Sage moaned, thinking about the eighteen-hour overnight bus ride ahead. "Oh, that's right. Playa del Carmen to Mexico City …we have to return to

173

the capital for our flight." She sighed. "We're leaving the country tomorrow."

"I can see this is a moment of sadness for you," Abril said. "Goodbyes are never easy. Have no fear. Mexico will remain with you forever. Without doubt."

"You will take *Compañia Autobuses de México* tonight," Fernando said. "It is a *very* good bus, the most comfortable in our country. Private rooms, with much comfort." Fernando cranked the ignition, and the motor coughed to life. A puff of smoke rose into the sky as the engine's purr grew into a mighty roar.

Sage sat in the rear and studied the boat's wake. She felt sad as the choppy Caribbean waters seemed to wave goodbye. *Our final night in Mexico*, she thought. *And we still haven't solved Frida's puzzle. We're stumped, and I don't know what to do next.*

Her sadness turned briefly to joy as she thought about the various messages etched into the tunnel of love. *Me encanta a Juan ... El amor de Carol y Cristobal.* She smiled as Abril's voice filled her head, *It is all about perspective ... timing ... and angle of the light.*

21

Wisdom, Love, and Illumination

Sage sat up in her bed, peeled the curtain back, and peeked out the bus window. Headlights jockeyed for position on the highway as vehicles raced alongside the motor coach. She closed the curtain, then stretched out on a cot. Her mom covered her with a blanket and sat at the foot of the bed, then reached into a bag and emerged with a wide-toothed wooden comb, paddle brush, bobby pins, a small jar of moisturizer, and a silk scarf. She opened the scarf, placed it atop the bed, and laid the bobby pins, comb, and brush on top.

"Listen, Sage." Her mom began unbraiding her thick hair. "I know your body's going through a lot of changes right now. Mentally, emotionally, physically ... this is all normal for a girl your age. And I know I'm just boring old Mom, but I'm always here if you want to talk about anything." She opened the moisturizer and began applying the soothing ointment to Sage's hair and scalp.

"Why *me*? Why *now*?"

"It's a part of life, dear. We all go through it ... some later than others." She grabbed several bobby pins and began inserting them into Sage's hair. "When we were in Mexico City, I was chatting with Manuel. We were talking about Beatriz."

"I love her! She's the nicest person I've ever met!"

"Yes, a sweetheart." She retrieved the scarf. "Sage ... when Beatriz was your age, and her body was maturing, she noticed something ... different. You see, when all her friends were experiencing these new changes—the same ones you are—Beatriz noticed that she wasn't. At first, she thought maybe it would just start later ... but then she told Manuel, and they visited a doctor."

"Mommy, what happened?"

"It's her reproductive organs, dear. A rare genetic disorder that ... Beatriz can't ... she isn't able to have children."

"That's awful! But you just mean ... for now, right? She can *later*."

"Her body isn't able to produce eggs, Sage. She'll never have children."

"I don't believe it." Then Sage remembered Beatriz's strange reaction during their tour of Frida's house. "So *that's* why she was so sad."

"Beatriz?"

Sage nodded. "I didn't know." She felt her eyes watering. "Mommy, I didn't know!"

"Shhh, of course you didn't." She wiped Sage's eyes. "And I'll tell you what else Manuel said. He told me that Beatriz absolutely *adores* you! She refers to you privately as her *pareja pequeña*. Do you know what that means?"

"Yes, Mommy." Sage giggled through her sniffles. "It's Spanish for *little bird*."

"My point, Sage, is that it's easy to see things in a negative light. I know your body's changing, but your *curse* would be Beatriz's *blessing*. Your body is preparing itself for the future, and we must remember to see things from the proper perspective." Her mom draped the scarf across Sage's head and tied it closed. She kissed Sage's forehead. "I'm always here for you, okay?"

"Yes, Mommy."

Sage's dad knocked on the door then poked a head inside. "Room for three in here?"

"I'm done, Bruce." She kissed Sage once more then stood up. "Gotta get ready for bed myself."

"That's fine, dear." He winked at Sage. "I can take it from here."

"Night, night, termite," her mom said before exiting.

"Goodnight, Mommy."

Sage's dad placed his hand on her back, then

leaned in and kissed the top of her scarfed head. "I love you, angel. More than you will ever know."

"I love you too, Daddy ... more than *you* will ever know." Her attention was drawn to a small metal plate below the window. It was the size of a stick of chewing gum. A passing car's headlights shined into the bus and illuminated the metal long enough for Sage to read the embossed words: *Compañia Autobuses de México*. Her thoughts shifted to the cipher she and Isabel had discovered at Chichen Itza. *Where does Frida want us to go to next?*

Her father's expression of love transformed into one of curiosity. "A penny for your thoughts?"

Sage snapped out of her daze. "What'd you say, Daddy?"

"Ever since you were a toddler, you've worn your heart on your sleeve ... and your emotions on your face. Something's on your mind."

How does he always do that? she wondered. *He never misses when I'm thinking super hard about a problem.*

She tried to wipe the heart off her sleeve and present a poker face. "There. How's that?"

"Nope, nice try though." He smiled. "Tell me something about yourself, Nefertari."

Nefertari? she thought. *He only calls me that when I'm in trouble (which I'm not!) or when he wants me to focus on what he's saying. This must be the second one.* She gave him her full attention. "What do you want to know?"

"Tell me something about yourself."

She knew that was all she'd get out of him until she responded. After thinking for a moment, she said the first things that popped into her mind. "Well ... I'm twelve years old—almost thirteen, really. I'm from Washington, DC. My favorite food is spaghetti. My favorite color is green." She could see in her father's eyes that she wasn't providing the information he was seeking. Nonetheless, she figured she'd continue until he interrupted and changed her direction. "My favorite sport is baseball. I love science and math and—"

"Tell me something more ... *Nefertari.*"

Sage smiled at the loving way he said her name. *Maybe* my name *is a clue to his lesson*, she thought. "I am Nefertari."

He nodded.

"I come from the source of the Nile River, at the foothills of the mountain of the moon." When her father's eyes softened, she knew she was moving down the correct path.

"What else?" he asked.

She searched her memory for the endless lessons her father had taught her about life. In her twelve years on Earth, Sage imagined she knew herself better than many who'd lived five times longer. She relaxed and began sharing the universal truths that her father had instilled within her. "I'm beautiful."

"What else?"

"I'm brilliant."

"Do you know who you are?"

"Yes, Daddy. I know who I am."

"Tell me who."

"I'm Nefertari, and I'm a child of God."

"And ..."

"And I love myself."

Her father leaned in. His piercing eyes sent a tingle down Sage's spine. He often looked at her in this way when he wanted to drive home important facts. "Are you 'beautiful *or* brilliant'?"

"No," Sage said with a nervous giggle.

"Why are you laughing?" he asked. "You don't believe yourself?"

Sage absolutely believed that she was brilliant. She just felt a little silly saying it out loud.

"When you mean something, Nefertari, you look people in the eye and you say it. You don't giggle. You don't apologize. And you don't back down." He maintained eye contact. "Understand?"

She felt a more confident energy fill her spirit, then looked into her father's eyes. "I'm beautiful *and* brilliant."

"Does that make you *better* than other people?"

"No, Daddy."

"Does that make you *less* than other people?"

"No, Daddy." She didn't fully understand how or where this newfound confidence was coming from, but she sensed that the words she was speaking had something to do with it. *Funny things, words*, she thought. *They sure are powerful.*

"Tell me again," her father said.

"I'm Nefertari. I come from the source of the Nile River. From the foothills of the mountain of the moon. I'm *beautiful*, and I'm *brilliant*." She felt the weight of her day melt away. The anxiety. The stress. The endless concern about solving Frida's cryptogram. Of course, she still wanted to decipher the message, but the heavy cloud of worry dissipated from her mind. She could see in her father's eyes that *this* was the lesson.

"I've always taught you … focus less on *what* you want to be and more on *who*. The *what* is a title, a social position. But the *who* is your character. *What* is how you appear in the presence of others. But *who* is—"

"*Who* is how I appear when no one else is around," she said.

He leaned in and kissed her head once more. "Whatever's on your mind … you'll figure it out, Nefertari, when you look at the situation from a different perspective. Life is all about your point of view." He touched her forehead. "You have it in here." He then placed his palm across her heart. "And in here. It's with you always."

Sage felt overwhelmed by her emotions. She didn't fully understand everything that her dad was saying, but she understood enough to realize that 'it' was her intelligence. Her confidence. Her strength. "Okay, Daddy." She sat up and wrapped both arms around his neck. "I love you."

"I love you too, princess. You have no idea."

As hard as she had fought against it, she finally decided to let herself cry in front of her dad. Several tears streamed down her cheeks as she closed her eyes and squeezed him tighter. "I *do* know, Daddy. Really, I do."

"Never forget, Nefertari."

At that moment, she wasn't sure if her dad was referring to his love for her or to her own knowledge of self. She supposed that he was most likely referring to both. She was always impressed with how he could speak to her on multiple levels at the same time. For as long as she remembered, he'd had a way of doing that. She simply chalked it up to *my incredible Daddy*. "I'll never forget. Promise."

He unraveled her arms from his neck and laid her back onto the mattress. "Time to rest, kiddo." He pulled the cover up to her chin. "Our final night in Mexico. We depart for New York City tomorrow, and then it's on to *Cidade Maravilhosa.*"

"What's that?"

"The nickname for Rio de Janeiro, sweetheart. *The Marvelous City.*"

"Don't you mean *Ciudad*? That's the Spanish word for 'city.'"

"No Spanish in Brazil, babe. The official language is Portuguese."

"Are you sure?"

He chuckled. "Absolutely. That reminds me ... I'll have to teach you some words and phrases."

"You speak Portuguese, Daddy?"

"*Mais ou menos.*"

"Cool!" Sage grinned. "Then that will be my next language! Wow, *three* languages. I'll be just like Frida!"

"We'll study later." He looked at his watch. "But for now, it's bedtime."

"*Buenas noches*, Daddy."

"Goodnight, princess."

As her father closed the door to her cabin, Sage laid her head on the pillow. She thought about Beatriz and remembered what she said on their first day in the Frida Kahlo Museum: *In life, we do not always receive what it is that we want.* Then her father's voice filled her head. *You'll figure it out, Nefertari, when you look at the situation from a different perspective. Life is all about your point of view ... different perspective ... point of view ... per-spective ... it's with you always.* She looked at the metallic plate below the window again. In the dim starlight, she couldn't see any details on its surface. It wasn't until another car's headlights entered the window and shined on the metal that the embossed words appeared: *Compañia Autobuses de México.*

"Wait a second!" Her heart skipped a beat as she remembered what Abril had said. *The Tunnel of Love ... I am happy you were able to see the notes. For now is the best time of the day for sunlight to reach ... it is all about perspective ... timing ... and the angle of the light.*

"The angle of the light."

A vision of Frida's cipher flashed into her mind. *Find me in the light.* Then Isabel's voice: *It's actually oblique light if you want to be exact ... Ms. Koonce's art class ... she shined her light parallel across the canvas ... that way, we could see every detail of the paint's texture.*

"Raking light," Sage said as Isabel's voice continued inside her head. *Sort of like how you can see dust particles in the air at sunset ... it's the sharp angle ... lots of details in oblique light that would otherwise be invisible ...*

"That's it!" She tossed her blanket off and jumped out of bed, then crept to the door, opened it,

184

and scream-whispered: "Izzy, I've got it!" Not hearing an answer, she tiptoed into the hallway. "Izzy! I know the answer to Frida's puzzle!"

22

Beyond the Surface

Sage sneaked down the hallway and gently knocked on Isabel's door. "Pssst! Izzy, you awake?" She knocked again. "Isabel. I figured it out!" As Sage turned the doorknob, it creaked loudly. "Shhh!" She whispered to herself before opening the door and slipping into Isabel's room.

"Izzy, are you sleeping? Isabel, I have to talk to you! I know where Frida wants us to look next!"

Isabel's eyes fluttered as she awoke. "Sage? What are you doing in here?"

"It's Frida."

"What about her?"

Sage caught her breath. "I know where the next clue is."

Isabel seemed to shake off her fatigue. "You do? Well ...where?"

"It's like you told me, Izzy. Four days ago on the plane in DC." She pointed to the metal plaque on

186

Isabel's window. "Remember?"

Isabel looked at the plaque but didn't seem to get Sage's point.

"It's like a ray of sunlight entering the window during sunset ... or a ray of light entering the Tunnel of Love in the Caribbean Sea ... or even a ray of light entering this bus in the middle of the night."

A passing car's headlights illuminated the metal sign under Sage's finger: *Compañia Autobuses de México*.

"What are you talking about, Sage-asaurus?" Isabel rubbed her eyes. "I ... I don't get it."

"Here, I'll show you!" She shuffled through several items on the floor: a small toolbox, rubber gloves, dust mask, and safety goggles. "Isabel ..." Sage picked up a hard hat. "Really?"

Isabel chuckled nervously. "Always be prepared."

"Where's your *End of World Kit?*"

Isabel rolled over. "Here." She retrieved the red backpack on the other side of her bed.

"You sleep with that thing?"

"Well not always ... I was just a little nervous tonight."

Izzy is sooo cute! "I need the *Book of Love* ... and your photos of *The Two Fridas* from our first day in Mexico. Oh, and a magnifying glass and flashlight."

Isabel reached into the bag and retrieved everything Sage asked for. "But ... why?"

Sage opened the *Book of Love* on the bed, then scattered Isabel's photos around it. "I noticed something that first day, Izzy, but I didn't realize it." She shined the flashlight on the pictures then hovered the magnifying glass over them in search of a photo from the correct angle. "I thought they were scratches, or maybe strokes of Frida's paint on the canvas." She found a photo that Isabel had shot from a close, parallel point of view. She stared through the magnifying glass, slowly moving it around the stitching of each Frida's dress in the photos. "But I missed the truth because I was looking *straight* at it ... and not from an angle. But *you* did ... with your macro lens. Look ..."

Isabel leaned in as Sage pointed to a collection of markings below the visible cryptogram they'd initially discovered. "Are those ..." She took the magnifying glass from Sage and leaned in for closer inspection. "Is this ..."

"Another cipher!"

"No way."

"Invisible to the eye in normal light. But visible in ..."

"Oblique light!"

"'Look again for the first time,' Frida said. She's talking about looking at the *painting* again, but from a different perspective."

You'll figure it out, Nefertari, she recalled her dad saying. *When you look at the situation from a different perspective. Life is all about your point of view.*

"A raking-light cipher?" Isabel said. "Does that even exist?"

"It's like Beatriz told us. Frida was a master of light."

"So she created two ciphers within the same space ... one visible ... and the other invisible."

Sage clicked off the flashlight and lowered the magnifying glass. "She was a genius."

"So what's our next move, Sage-asaurus?"

"We have to return to Casa Azul for a closer look at Frida's raking-light cryptogram. We're so close, Izzy."

"But our flight! We're out of time. I hate to admit it, but Benji was right. The wild-goose chase is over."

"We can't give up! We have to at least try. What if we never return to Mexico? Then we'll never solve Frida's puzzle."

Isabel exhaled, thinking, then nodded. "You're right. We have to give it our best shot."

"Yes!" Sage hugged Isabel.

"But how do we get more time?"

"I have to talk to my dad." Sage found more confidence as she continued talking. "And tell him about *The Two Fridas,* the ciphers ... everything. Then I'll explain how we want to return to her museum for one final look before leaving the country."

"You're gonna tell your dad our secret!?"

Sage thought about her conversation with Aunt Drusilla. *Share what's on your mind, Bird. No need to keep everything secret.* "Sunlight is the best disinfectant, Izzy-dactyl. Didn't you know that?"

"Huh?"

"Everything doesn't have to be so hush-hush. We can ask for help when we're not sure about some things."

"Sunlight is the best disinfectant," Isabel repeated. "Hmmm, must be the ultraviolet waves, you know, biologically speaking. I'll bet the radiation kills bacteria. I sure wish I could stash some rays inside my *End of World Kit.* I can always use another disinfectant."

"Always be prepared." Sage stood and made her way to the door, then yawned. "I feel like we haven't slept in a week."

Isabel laughed. "We haven't!"

"Get some rest, Izzy. We'll need it. Tomorrow, we *finally* solve Frida's mystery ... with our parents' help."

"I can't wait!"

"Me too." Sage crept out of Isabel's room. As she

tiptoed down the hallway, she felt like a massive weight had been lifted off her back. Drusilla's voice filled her head again. *Nothing stays the same forever, babe. The only constant in life is change.* "I understand now, Aunt Dru. I understand."

23

Return to Casa Azul

"Get out of the way!" Sage shouted at the masses of cars, trucks, and bicycles jamming the streets of Mexico City. "We've got important things to do!"

"Sage!" her mom said. "What's gotten into you?"

"Mommy, we have to get to Frida's house!"

"We're on our way, dear. But you know how the traffic is. We saw it earlier this week. And we're seeing it again today."

"Sit back," her dad said. "And put on your seat belt."

"But—"

"Seat belt!" he repeated.

"Awww, man." She leaned back and buckled up.

The van weaved across several lanes of traffic, picking up some speed. "Yes!" Sage said from the backseat, enjoying the urgency in their driver.

"So what's the plan for when we get to Frida's house?" Benji asked.

"We need to get a closer look at Frida's raking-light message." Sage opened the *Book of Love* and retrieved Isabel's photo. "There's more ciphertext here. So we need to examine it, then decrypt it."

"Decrypt it?" Benji repeated. "Do we have time?

Sage watched through the windshield as the van roared around a corner, and the Blue House appeared at the end of the block. The driver pointed to the end of the block. "Casa Azul is there."

Mr. Flores looked at his watch. "You have ten minutes. *¿Comprende?*"

"Yes, Daddy!" Isabel said.

As they approached, Sage smiled at the familiar green door leading into the house's courtyard, '*Museo Frida Kahlo*' painted on the bricks above.

Mr. Flores pressed a couple of buttons on his watch. "Ten minutes," he said with a smile. "And then we're leaving with or without you!"

As Sage hopped out of the van and raced toward the museum, she turned to Isabel. "Is your dad serious?"

Isabel laughed. "He's joking!"

The girls dashed into the museum, across the atrium, down the hallway, through a couple of galleries, and finally arrived at *The Two Fridas*. Moments later, Benji joined them, unwilling to let the girls have all the fun.

Sage looked at the two faces gazing back at her. "We're back, Frida. Just like you wanted."

"Ten minutes!" Isabel said, snapping Sage back into reality.

Sage crept in and located the coded message. "I need your magnifying glass, Izzy. And the flashlight."

"Here you go!"

Sage shined the light parallel to the painting. As she leaned in, the canvas's textures came to life. In the raking rays of the flashlight, she gazed through the magnifying glass. "I ... I see it! I see the cipher-text!"

Isabel tossed her backpack onto the floor, dug inside, and retrieved the *Book of Love* and a pen. She knelt to the ground and found a blank page. "What's it say!?"

Sage scanned the now-visible cipher and recited each symbol as Isabel furiously wrote inside the journal. "Okay, that's all of it!"

"We already have the cipher key," Benji said, looking at his watch. "And only four more minutes until Mr. Flores tells the van to leave us!"

"My dad won't leave us, Benji!"

Sage knelt beside Isabel as they began decoding the message. *We're so close! We're going to solve it!*

"This is an E," Isabel said. "And these are all T's."

"And here ... 2/10 and 3/15 are both equivalent. So they both break down to 1/5. That means they're all R's."

"Just a few more letters and we've got it!"

"Guys! We only have three minutes until they leave us!"

"Benji, please!"

"Yeah, Benji-raptor. Nobody's leaving anybody!"

He finally knelt beside the girls as Sage scribbled the missing letters into the book. "So, what's it say?"

She spun the booklet for a better look as Isabel retrieved her camera from the backpack and snapped several pictures. Sage slowly read the plaintext. *"Vuelve al Zócalo y encuéntrame, asta de la bandera verde, blanco, y rojo."*

Isabel continued photographing the scene while translating Sage's words. "Return to Zocalo and find me until the green, white, and red flag."

"*Until* the flag?" Benji said. "What does that mean?"

Sage continued reading the text. "*Saludo al cielo...*"

"I wave to the sky..."

"*Por encima del Distrito Federal ...*"

"Above the Federal District ... Frida."

"That's the whole message," Sage said. She thought back to their first day in Mexico City, and the National Palace, the Angel of Independence, and the Zocalo's massive flag. "Frida's final clue is on the flag!"

Isabel lowered her camera. "We have to go there!"

"But how are we going to look at the flag?" Benji said. "Let's be realistic, guys. We can't just walk into the Zocalo and take it down!"

"Sage! Isabel!" several adults shouted from the street. They were accompanied by the van's honking horn.

The kids gathered their belongings and stuffed everything into Isabel's bag. As they dashed out of the room, Sage turned for one final look at *The Two Fridas*. She recalled her first impressions of the painting four days ago: the beauty and strength of Frida's gazes. She then smiled at the amazing journey that she'd experienced with her friends and all of the people she'd met: Beatriz, Manuel, Escarlet, Victor, Fernando, and Abril.

"Come, on Sage-asaurus! I *never* outrun you!" Isabel grabbed Sage's arm and pulled her along as they exited the museum.

Benji's watch beeped. "Oh no, we're out of time. They're going to leave us!"

"Relax." Isabel pointed to the street. "See, there they are!"

The van's door slid open as they arrived. Sage hopped in then leaned forward. "We have to stop at the Zocalo!"

"What?" Mrs. Carrington said. "Why?"

"Frida's crypotgram, Daddy."

"Yeah, Mr. C, this is it. The final piece of her puzzle."

Sage's dad looked at his watch. "We're cutting it *very* close, guys. That plane isn't going to wait for us, you know."

"Well I think we should let them find out where this whole Frida story ends," Drusilla said. "Besides, it's not the last flight in history."

Sage saw her dad look at her mom, then at Isabel's parents. "Okay, we can stop by the Zocalo on the way. But just for a minute!"

"Yes!"

"Awesome!"

Mrs. Flores leaned over. "What did you find in there, anyway?"

"More symbols at the bottom of the painting, Mommy. But we deciphered them." Isabel reached into her backpack and retrieved the *Book of Love*. She opened the journal and extended it. "See ..."

Mrs. Flores examined the plaintext in the book. "La bandera ... verde, blanca, y rojo ... the green, white, and red flag."

"We think the final clue is written on the flag, Mrs. Flores. Maybe we can use Isabel's telephoto lens to see—"

"I'm not too sure about that, Sage." Mrs. Flores pointed to the Spanish text then to the English translation. "This part, dear. 'Until the green, white, and red flag.' That's not correct."

Isabel leaned in. "Are you sure, Mommy?"

Mrs. Flores nodded. "Look at the Spanish. "*Asta de la bandera.*'"

"Oh, it's *asta* with an A! I was taking pictures and never read the cipher. I thought Sage said *hasta* with an H!"

Benji shrugged. "Does that make any difference?"

"Absolutely!" Isabel said. "*Asta de la bandera* means flagpole!"

Sage's heart raced. "So Frida's final message isn't written on the *flag* ... it's written on the *flag-pole!*" She hugged Izzy in excitement. "Thanks, Mrs. Flores!"

"Yeah, thanks, Mommy!"

"Anytime. See, we old farts *can* be useful sometimes!"

"Well, it's a good thing we showed you, then." Sage reached a hand to the front seat and rubbed Drusilla's shoulder. "You know, sunlight *is* the best disinfectant."

Drusilla nodded. "Words of wisdom, Bird."

Sage now had the last piece of the puzzle. All that remained was a quick stop by the Zocalo to finally solve Frida's mystery.

24

Message on a Flagpole

"Get out of the way!" Sage once again shouted at the sea of traffic ahead. "I told you before ... we have important things to do!"

"Sage!" her mom said, this time less shocked by Sage's impatience. "What did I tell you about that?"

"All these cars and trucks, Mommy." Sage waved her arms side to side like she was trying to part the ocean. "They need to move."

Before Mrs. Carrington could respond, the driver jumped in. "*El Zócalo* is in one block." He pointed ahead. "*Ésta próximo.*"

Sage unfastened her seatbelt and prepared to hop out of the vehicle. She tapped Isabel on the arm. "You ready?"

Izzy was already tightening the straps on her backpack. "Got the *Book of Love*, the deciphered message, and a new roll of film locked and loaded." She tapped her camera. "Gonna go with my 50 mil, 1.4. Plus, I'm using super-fast ASA 1600 film."

The technical talk sailed over Sage's head; none-theless, she was reassured by Izzy's beaming smile and confident energy. "*¡Perfecto!*" As the van sped around a corner, Sage looked out the window and spotted the National Palace. "We're here!" she announced as Isabel flung open the door.

"Let's go!" Isabel hopped out and started jogging toward the center of the city square.

Mr. Flores pressed a couple of buttons on his watch. "Five minutes, and then we're leaving!" He laughed as he said it, as if he realized he was repeating himself.

Sage dashed across the Zocalo, then caught a glimpse of the Angel of Independence.

"Over here!" Benji shouted, sprinting to the flag-pole. Just as it had four days ago, the fabric flapped in the gusty winds of the Mexican capital.

"Hurry up, guys!" Sage dashed past Benji and Isabel, and fixed her gaze on the base of the flag-pole. The waving fabric seemed to glow in the warm evening light.

"Wait for me!" Sage heard Benji yell from behind. "Hey, slow down!"

Eleven year olds, Sage thought. *What are they ever good for?* Suddenly, a brisk breeze ripped across the Zocalo and nearly sent her tumbling to the concrete. She held up a hand to shield her face.

Crack! Crack!

The huge flag whipped overhead, its deafening flaps drawing her attention. She looked down and noticed that she was running beside the long shadow of the flagpole. *Oblique light of the setting sun*, she thought before finally arriving at the flagpole. "Okay, guys, let's find that final clue."

She squatted for a closer look at the flagpole's base, then noticed a small metal plaque. At first glance, it appeared to be blank. She rubbed her fingers across the metal and felt the texture of engraved marks. She smiled at the discovery. "Good one, Frida!"

Isabel arrived and knelt beside her. She removed her backpack and unzipped the main compartment. "What do you see, Sage-asaurus? Did you solve it yet?"

Sage examined the details around the plate. "This is it, Izzy-dactyl—Frida's final clue!" She motioned to Isabel's backpack. "I'll need the flashlight again."

Isabel retrieved the light and handed it to Sage. She then grabbed the *Book of Love* and prepared to write the latest symbols.

The sound of approaching footsteps gave way to Benji, who was gasping for air as he finally arrived. "What ... did ... you ... find? Did ... you ... solve ... the ... cipher?" He plopped onto the ground to catch his breath.

"Guys! I think I ... yes! I see something!"

Isabel tapped the pen on the paper. "So what's it say!?"

Benji's watch beeped. "Oh no! We're out of time!" He stood up, and a gust of wind nearly knocked him over. "Just forget it, guys. Let's go!"

Sage yanked his arm, bringing him back to the ground. "Not yet. We can't leave until we solve Frida's cipher."

"But we're going to miss our flight! We're *all* gonna miss the flight."

Sage knew that he could be right, but she also knew that the mystery was more important. "Two minutes, Benji. That's all we need."

"For sure." Isabel pointed to the metal plate then prepared to write. "So what do you see, Sage-asaurus?"

25

Frida's Final Words

Isabel and Benji perched their chins on Sage's shoulders.

Sage shined the light and leaned in, nearly touching her nose to the flagpole. "I see ... something. But it's so tiny! Izzy, do you have the magnifying glass?"

Isabel spun around and dove into the backpack. "Yep, it's here somewhere. I know it is." She tossed the bag's contents onto the ground: bottled water, freeze-dried food, and a small gas mask. "Found it!" She emerged with the magnifying glass. "Here you go!"

Benji's watch started beeping again. Sage's heart sank; she knew what that sound meant.

"We have to go!" he shouted as a vicious wind swept across the Zocalo.

The gust ripped the magnifying glass out of Isabel's hand and sent it tumbling to the concrete.

Its glass shattered. "Oh no!" Isabel scrambled to collect the shards. "The wind was so strong ... I just—"

Another gust roared along the ground. Papers, plastic bags, and other unattached debris pummeled the kids.

"We have to get out of here!" Benji yelled above the howling wind. "Our flight!"

"There's no way can we leave," Sage responded. "We're too close now!" She examined the flagpole again. "What do you want to tell us, Frida?" She shook her head. "These symbols are just too small. I need something to magnify..." Suddenly set her sights on ... "Benji!" she said. "Give me your glasses!"

"What? Wh-why?"

"Just give me your glasses. No time!"

The wind howled as he removed his specs and handed them to Sage. "Be careful. That's my only pair!"

Sage nodded. *Okay,* she thought, *so eleven year olds* are *helpful sometimes. Maybe.*

"What are you doing?" he asked. "I can't see anything."

Sage lowered his glasses to the metal plate, and, in the twilight, she inspected the magnified characters. Several letters came into focus. "It's in Spanish! No ciphertext!"

"What's it say, Sage-asaurus!?" Isabel grabbed the *Book of Love* and fanned through its pages.

"*Fel ... i ... cita ... ciones,*" Sage said.

"*Felicitaciones,*" Isabel repeated while writing inside the journal. "That means 'congratulations!'"

"*Eres verdadero descifrador de códigos ...*"

"You are a true ... code breaker... "

"*Mis palabras finales ...*"

"My final words ..."

"*Nunca te olvides que eres especial ...*"

"Never forget," Isabel said. "That you are special."

Another blast of air swept across the Zocalo as Sage continued., "*Yo se estar diferente ...*"

Isabel leaned an elbow on the book to keep it from blowing away. "I know what it is to be different."

"*Sin embargo,*" Sage said, "*por la vida ...*"

"Nonetheless, through life ..."

"*Voy como soy, y tu también debes.*"

"I go as I am." Isabel looked at Sage and smiled. "And you should too."

Sage returned the smile before a wall of debris pelted the plaza.

"Is that the end of the message?" Benji yelled. "We're gonna miss the flight!"

"Just a couple more lines." Sage returned her attention to the message. "*Siempre ámate como ningún más. Es el mejor amor en todo mundo ...*"

"Always love yourself like no one else," Isabel said. "This is the best love in the world."

"*Con cariño. Hija orgullosa de México ...*"

"With affection ... proud daughter of Mexico ..."

"She signed it with a heart and star."

Isabel gasped. "Ciphertext!"

Sage nodded as she remembered the letters for these two shapes: F and K.

"Is that all of it?"

Sage lowered the magnifying glass. "That's all, Izzy."

Benji raised both arms. "We did it!"

We found your cryptogram, Sage thought. *We solved your mystery, Frida.* The brisk winds subsided, and a tranquil energy blanketed the Zocalo. *And I know your spirit is here with us.*

"So, it's all over now?" Isabel seemed sad as she returned the journal to her backpack.

Sage understood what her friend was asking. For the past four days, the mysterious pursuit had consumed them. The thrill of this chase occupied their thoughts. And now it was done. "Yeah," she admitted. "It's over."

"We cracked the code." Benji snatched his glasses from Sage. "Thanks to me!"

Technically he was correct, and Sage knew it. After all, it was *his* glasses that allowed her to read Frida's final secret message. "*Gracias*, Benji."

He froze, waiting for more.

"Fine." Sage cleared her throat. "We ... couldn't have done it without you, Benji-raptor."

"Yes!" He hopped into the air. "You're welcome, Sage-asaurus." They high-fived. "And you too, Izzy-dactyl."

Sage flashed a grin, then clutched Isabel's arm as the two began trotting back to the van.

Benji trailed, his newfound heroism on full display. "Hey, we make a good team, huh? I mean the three of us. Like a trio. We all help one another. And did you see that wind? Boy, it sure was strong. But at least we had my glasses to figure out the ..."

His voice faded into the background as Sage imagined how Frida assembled all these pieces of her great mystery. Decades ago, she must have carefully planned the puzzle while her husband Diego worked on the mural in the National Palace ... and the plates in Chichen Itza and here at the flagpole in the Zocalo. She continued jogging to the van, thinking of Frida's eyes and hands engraving the various messages into the metal. "We *did* it."

Isabel glanced at Sage and sent a smile. "We did it!"

The girls arrived at the shuttle, and as the vehicle's door slid open, they jumped inside.

"Where's Benjamin?" Mrs. Flores asked.

Benji arrived and hopped in. "We figured it out! We saw her final message. And it was all because of me! They really needed my help and I ..." The door closed, and the van's engine roared to life.

As Benji continued, Sage saw her dad glance at his watch. "This is gonna be close," he said.

Sage looked at Isabel and Benji. They all smiled at one another. Then she saw the worried looks on the adults' faces. *Now we just need to make our flight!*

26

Airport Dash

"Get out of the way!" Mrs. Carrington shouted through the windshield. "How many times do we have to say it ... we've got important things to do!"

"Mommy!" Sage said, surprised at how her mom was displaying the same impatience she had earlier.

Her mom didn't seem to be in the mood for silence. "All these cars and trucks!" She glanced at her watch. "We *can't* miss our flight." She waved her arms side to side as if trying to part the ocean. "Get out of the way!"

Sage felt a little nervous. After all, it was because of her and her friends that everyone was racing around the city in the first place. Frida's Museum, the Zocalo ... if it weren't for those stops, then the team would already be sitting in the airport terminal, waiting to board the plane. She decided to give her mother some help. "You heard what my mom said." She waved her arms as well. "Move it!"

The van swerved from lane to lane as a chorus of car horns littered the air.

Whoosh!

A jumbo jet soared overhead, its massive wings slicing through the sky. *That plane's pretty low.* Sage thought. *We must be close to the airport!* She leaned forward to gaze through the windshield ...

Whoosh!

Another jet flew by. This time she could see its landing gear open; its wheels were preparing for touchdown. The van screeched around a corner, then toward a ramp with a sign that read *Aeropuerto Internacional Benito Juárez.*

"We made it!" Sage announced.

Mr. Flores looked at his watch. "Maybe, Sage. But we still need to get through security."

"Oh no! I forgot about security!" Images of a mile-long line filled her head. "Well, we can *still* make it. Anything's possible."

Mrs. Carrington chirped. "We'll need a miracle."

Sage thought of Frida's cryptogram and how she and her friends had solved the impossible puzzle. "Miracles happen every day, Mommy."

"How much time do we have?" Isabel asked.

Mrs. Flores responded. "About forty-five minutes."

"Grab your bags, everyone," Mr. Carrington said. "This'll be a race to the gate!"

The passengers scrambled out of the van, snatched their bags, and dashed into the terminal.

"Let's go!" Mr. Flores yelled. He kicked the bottom of his suitcase and tilted it onto a set of wheels. "Last one to the gate is a *huevo podrido*."

Benji shouted, "A what?"

"A rotten egg!" Isabel said.

Sage grabbed Benji's hand. "Just run!"

27

Race to the Gate

Automatic doors slid open, and Sage felt a refreshing rush of air. Mexico's warm evening had surrendered to the cold filtered air of the terminal's ventilation system.

"This way!" Mr. Flores yelled as he raced straight ahead. Sage saw a sign above his head: *International Departures.* "Security checkpoint's right here."

Her dad trotted ahead of Mr. Flores and turned a corner. "I don't believe it!" he said. "Incredible!"

Sage's heart sank at her dad's surprise. *Oh no! The line must be wrapped around the building.* But then she raced around the corner herself and saw her dad placing his bags in the security scanner already.

"Incredible!" Mr. Carrington repeated. "Nobody's in line!" He motioned for Sage to come closer, and tossed her bag onto the conveyor belt. "Go on through, honey."

Sage tiptoed closer to the security agent, who waved her through a large doorframe-looking device. Sage's pulse raced for a moment as she anticipated a piercing alarm followed by SWAT agents descending from the ceiling. *We can still make the plane. Please, no sirens!* She stepped through—no alarm—and emerged on the other side, then collected her bag from the conveyor and waited for the others to join.

Her parents hopped through security with no problems. Mr. and Mrs. Flores joined Isabel as they also cleared the screening. Benji tossed his bag onto the conveyor then strutted through the doorframe.

Beep. Beep. Beep.

"Please remove your belt, sir," the security agent said. "Also any metal objects in your pockets."

"I—I don't have a belt ... or any metal objects," Benji said.

"Please hold your arms out like this," the agent said while illustrating.

Benji complied as the agent waved a thick plastic wand around Benji's body. The wand arrived at Benji's face and ...

Beep. Beep. Beep.

The agent tapped Benji's glasses. "Do you have metal frames?"

Benji's eyes lit up. "Oh! I forgot! He removed his glasses, handed them to the agent, and re-entered the screening machine. He released a chuckle while maneuvering past the security agent. "I forgot! Promise!"

"It's okay, sir. Enjoy your flight."

Our flight! Sage helped Benji collect his bag while Aunt Drusilla strolled through security without issue. Finally, the whole team had made it.

Mr. Carrington looked at his watch. "Fifteen minutes until departure!"

"The gate's over there!" Mrs. Flores announced.

Sage saw a man and woman standing at the counter. The door to board the airplane was still open, and a sign flashed above their heads: *NEW YORK—ON TIME.* "We made it!" she said.

"Without much time to waste." The gate agent smiled. "We're to close this door in two minutes." She stepped aside and extended an arm toward the airplane. "Would you like to travel to New York City this evening?"

The group wasted no time responding.

"Yes!"

"*¡Sí!*"

"Absolutely!"

"*Entonces.*" The agent waved the group through. "*¡Buen viaje!*"

"*¡Gracias!*"

"*¡Muchas gracias!*"

As they stampeded down the boarding tunnel, Sage turned and watched the agents close the door behind them. *That was close,* she thought. *We just* barely *made it.*

28

Ready for Arrival

"*Buenas noches, damas y caballeros.* This is your captain speaking. We are next in line to depart for New York City. The night is clear, and we expect a smooth flight. Dinner service is available, after reaching our cruising altitude. One more thing ... even though we are traveling to the City That Never Sleeps, we encourage you to do the opposite. Pillows are under your seats, so please sit back, relax, and get some rest. We'll arrive in New York in the morning."

Sage reached into the seat pocket in front of her and retrieved an airline magazine. As she had four days ago in Washington, DC, she showed the bilingual articles to Isabel.

"Your Spanish is *excelente* now, Sage-asaurus. *Muy bueno.*" She laid her head on Sage's shoulder.

"*Gracias, mi amiga.*" After replacing the magazine, Sage retrieved the *Book of Love* and flipped through the journal. She located the flagpole notes from Frida and smiled while reading the final message. *Voy como soy. Y tu también debes.* "I go as I am ..." She yawned, then returned the journal to the seat pocket. "And you should too." She noticed a small metallic plate attached to the seatback and poked Isabel's arm. "Raking light ..."

Isabel pried an eye open to see what Sage was referring to. "Or oblique ... if you want to be exact." She yawned, then closed her eyes again. "Ms. Koonce ... National Gallery of Art ..."

Sage felt her body pressing against the seat as the runway's lights began to race past her window. She was happy and sad at the same time. She'd had an incredible journey across Mexico. The beautiful country had welcomed her with open arms and, as she was leaving, a powerful realization swept over her.

"Four days ago, Izzy, when we were in the airport terminal, I imagined visiting the Mayan temples and the Olmec statues, and I thought about all the beautiful beaches we'd see. I dreamed about my SCUBA dive and Frida's paintings. But there's one thing I forgot to calculate—something missing from all the pamphlets and tour books: *the people.* Beatriz, Manuel, Abril, Fernando, Escarlet, Victor ... traveling isn't about the things and the places ... it's really about the people, and that's the hardest part. We *just* met them, and now we're already leaving. I just … I want to stay in touch, you know?"

She looked out the window and smiled at a glorious sunset. *So beautiful,* she thought as the fiery sun sank into the horizon. "You know, Izzy, my grandma would always tell me, 'Never say goodbye, because that's too final,' like we'll never meet again. So I won't say *adios* either. Instead, I'll say *hasta luego.* Because we'll all see each other again."

On the other side of her sadness, Sage discovered tremendous joy. She knew they were going to Brazil, but not until *after* spending a few days in New York City—two places that she had always dreamed of visiting. Her imagination overflowed with visions of Central Park, skyscrapers, Broadway, and street musicians playing for pennies on the corner. And then *Cidade Maravillosa*—Samba music, beaches, and Portuguese. *Imagine all the* … people *we'll meet!* "The Big Apple," she whispered. "Izzy, can you believe it!?"

But Isabel was fast asleep.

Did she hear anything *I just said?* Sage giggled to herself. "*Buenas noches,* Izzy-dactyl. And goodnight Abril, Fernando, Victor, Escarlet, Manuel, Beatriz … and *Frida.*"

The harsh bumps of the runway disappeared as the airplane took flight, and Beatriz's voice filled Sage's head. *The world is a book, and those who do not travel read only a page. Well then,* Sage thought,

I guess it's time to turn a new page. I wonder who we'll meet in New York. And if the city has any mysteries. She covered Isabel with a blanket then closed her eyes. *We'll find out ... in the morning.*

About the Author

Justin Scott Parr was born and raised in Greensboro, North Carolina. An adventurer at heart, he imparts his love of "the journey" into each Sage Carrington tale. "My first international travel was to Africa," he says, "the Nile Valley of Egypt. That voyage changed my life by awakening a deep historical curiosity. Since then, I've accumulated wisdom from myriad travel experiences, and I want to help kids learn about the various cultures and vibrant locales that make our world such an incredible place." Mr. Parr lives in New York City.

Sage Carrington

Made in the USA
Middletown, DE
22 October 2017